ME & MY
INVISIBLE
GUY

ME & MY
INVISIBLE
GUY

SARAH JEFFREY

AMAZON CHILDREN'S PUBLISHING

Text copyright © 2013 by Sarah Jeffrey

Amazon Publishing
Attn: Amazon Children's Publishing
P.O. Box 400818
Las Vegas, NV 89140
www.amazon.com/amazonchildrenspublishing

Library of Congress Cataloging-in-Publication Data is available.

9781477816363 (hardcover)
1477816364 (hardcover)
9781477866368 (eBook)
1477866361 (eBook)

Book design by Becky Terhune
Editor: Marilyn Brigham

Printed in the United States of America (R)
First edition
10 9 8 7 6 5 4 3 2 1

TO MY HUSBAND:
MY BEST FRIEND
MY FOREVER LOVE

CHAPTER 1

"Hi. My name is Mallory Dane, and I am a liar."

I scowled into the mirror to make the reprimand more potent. Admitting that I was powerless over my lying was supposedly the first step, but repeating it in front of the mirror hadn't helped at all. I'd been doing it every morning for at least a month, and I still hadn't even come close to confessing to an actual human.

It would be too . . . complicated.

Complicated—that was an understatement. It would be fraught with complications, or, in a nod to the evil SAT, "replete" with complications.

My eyes drifted to a picture of Todd and me stuck to the top corner of my mirror, courtesy of the fabulous Photoshop. There were days when I looked at that picture of us—the beach in the background, the sky turning a soft orange— and I almost believed it really happened. That some random passerby had offered to take a picture of us together, and we smiled—our image captured.

But today I didn't even bother trying to pretend it was real or to conjure up details of our silly fight and instead remembered sitting in front of my computer, cutting and pasting us together. I was tired of him and all the problems that came with him. I wanted a real life.

"Mallory!" Mom opened my door. "Where is she?"

1

"In her room." *Hello to you, too, Mom.*

"Did you check on her?"

I grabbed a brush from my dresser, refusing to look at my mother. "Of course."

She left without a word, leaving the door ajar. I wanted to slam it shut. I wanted to—but I didn't. I was too well trained. I just closed it and leaned against it.

Today was not the day for confessions.

Tess texted me and said she was coming over to use my computer. It would be useless to refuse, so I threw some clothes into a bag and rushed downstairs to intercept her.

Mom was at the kitchen table grading papers. "Dad will be ready to leave soon," she said.

"Okay."

Her hair was falling out of her ponytail, and her glasses kept slipping. It reminded me so much of how she was before that I thought about hugging her. But I didn't do that either.

Tess pounded on the door, making Mom jump. "Mallory, be sure that . . ."

I walked away before she could finish and opened the door for Tess. I love Tess. Years ago we had a visiting speaker come to our school and yammer at us about being nice to one another and forging authentic support systems. I couldn't remember much of what he said except that we all need a "safe place" to go when things are hard. Tess has always been my safe place.

"What's wrong?" Tess put her hand on her hip.

"Nothing."

She scowled. "Yeah. And I'm the next American Idol."

Tess walked past me, and I followed her up to my room.

She sat at the computer and started typing and scrolling.

"When are you coming home? I think Yvie is having a party tomorrow night."

"Not till Sunday."

Tess turned and looked at the bag, which I'd thrown on my bed. "Going to see Todd?"

Todd. Yes, always Todd.

I put a smile on my face. "Only tonight, I think. He has a . . . thing tomorrow."

"You'll be back in time for the party?"

"No, I'm staying over with my grandmother."

Tess shrugged and turned back to the computer. "I think you're the only sixteen-year-old on the planet who spends so much time with her grandmother."

"It's my last weekend before football starts. And I have to leave in a few minutes," I reminded her.

"Sorry. Let me send these e-mails. You know I love you, right?"

Tess doesn't have Internet or even a computer at her house, so she's constantly borrowing mine. I didn't usually mind, but it made things tricky sometimes.

"You have to help me decide which fund-raiser. These are the last two packets I have to order, and I think I'll have every possibility known to humankind. You'll call me when you get back so we can talk?"

"Of course."

"Okay. I'll let you have your last Todd weekend. Then it's football and cheering and parties. And if Todd can't get his butt here for some of it—*especially* homecoming—I'll have to have a few words with him myself."

"I believe that."

I hurried Tess out the door, but getting past Mom was much harder.

Dad and I loaded all the equipment, but Mom stopped me before I got in the driver's seat. "You should say good-bye to Darby," she said.

"We have to go, Amy," Dad said. He sounded more exhausted than upset.

"Look. We don't know what can happen. What if you get back and . . ." She couldn't say it, and I didn't want to hear it.

I closed the door. "I'll go. I'm going." I could hear them arguing behind me all the way to the front door. I took the stairs two at a time and then stood at Darby's closed door for a long moment, thinking about what my mom didn't say.

I knocked lightly and pushed open the door.

Darby was curled up in her Papasan chair with a textbook open in her lap. She was in her pajama pants and college sweatshirt, and her hair was twisted into a messy bun on top of her head. I had always seen Darby as strong and beautiful. Able to do anything.

She didn't look strong to me anymore. More like she might fall apart at any moment.

"Dad and I are heading out. Thought I'd say good-bye."

"Have fun." Darby's words were cheery. They didn't match what her eyes told me.

"Okay, well, good luck with your studying."

"Thanks."

I closed the door and hurried back to the SUV.

Mom and Dad were still arguing, so I climbed in the driver's seat and shut the door. I checked my texts. Two from Tess asking me to reconsider coming back in time for the party. One from Sophie telling me not to have so much fun that I come home pregnant.

I turned off the phone and threw it in my backpack.

When Dad finally got in, I pulled out of the driveway quickly and headed north. Away from home.

I could feel myself relax with every mile we drove away. It was a perfect day. Warm sun, blue sky dotted with puffy white clouds, and miles of open countryside. Even though Dad and I had been to the winery for a wedding before, we took a road that was forty-five miles out of the way so that we could look for barns. There was something about broken-down barns in a pretty field that made both of us want to take a picture.

We didn't talk about home. We never did. Even when things were worse, and they *had* been worse, Dad and I had an unspoken contract to enjoy every moment of our escape.

We were almost back to the main highway when I saw a rotting gray barn in a field off to my right. I slowed down and made a hard turn onto a gravel trail, kicking up dirt and debris from the tires. Dad grabbed his laptop and held it to his chest, and laughed.

I parked the SUV, and we both grabbed our cameras and walked toward the barn.

It towered three stories high, and the area around it was littered with rusting metal farm equipment and other debris. We each took our own pictures until Dad started posing me in various positions, close-up and far away. Dad had me sit with my arms stretched out behind me in a patch of sunlight.

Later, I could Photoshop Todd into one or two of the pictures. Do some fake status updates, and my weekend away would be documented. My fake trip. My fake life.

Dad waved me back and hurried me into the car so that we could do what we really came to do. Shoot the wedding of Diana and Alfred Grey at the Lake Anna Winery.

I began shooting weddings and working with my dad's photography business when I was twelve. Originally, he'd just needed an extra hand to do the photo booth and carry the equipment. But then I began learning the software and helped him with the digital design of the photos. I took candids and other shots of the wedding, but I also took shots of the overall design aesthetic and then used the colors and textures to create . . . well, whatever the couple wanted. I made digital albums, collages, digital backdrops to use behind the posed portraits, and anything I was inspired to make.

We were a team. A pretty good one.

I glanced at my dad, who had his laptop open, and wondered if he liked escaping as much as I did. Of course, it was different for him; this was his job.

Being his assistant had its perks. One of them was watching him work a wedding. Dad could pose group after group and coax even the most ambivalent groomsman into giving him the picture he was looking for. Every shot he needed was planned in advance, and he was swift and effective. At the reception he was like a ghost, moving through the party, capturing images that I would marvel at later, while never interrupting the party.

He was so different at weddings than he was at home. At a wedding he orchestrated everything like a master conductor. At home, well, he was just the ghost—always aware of what was going on but unwilling to disrupt the flow of events.

He smiled at me, a smile that told me, yeah, he loved escaping, too.

The wedding was lush and beautiful. The reception went on long after midnight, and by the time Dad and I got to our hotel room, we were both too exhausted to do anything but fall into bed. I didn't touch my phone, knowing there would be texts to deal with.

In the morning we drove home, barreling sixty miles an hour back toward reality.

Dad gave me a smile when he caught me looking at him. But it was a tight one, a weary one, and I knew I wasn't the only one who didn't want to leave.

Saturday would be spent dodging texts and laying low so that no one would know I was back home. Maybe Photoshopping so that I could text pictures, which was much harder than posting online.

Mom was at the door, already anxious, when we pulled into the garage.

"We have to leave for the picnic in less than an hour," she said to my dad. "I thought you'd be home earlier." Mom walked to the back of the SUV and yanked on the handle.

"We're home an hour earlier than I told you," Dad said, looking at his watch. He started unloading bags, ignoring the withering look my mom gave him.

"Sorry. I'm kind of tired, though. It was a long wedding, and we didn't get much sleep. Do you think I can skip this one?"

"Janelle is expecting both of us. I already confirmed it with her," Mom said.

I shoved all my stuff into my backpack and hurried inside.

I closed the door to my room and checked my phone. I wasn't going to answer anyone until I was technically back home. I thought about offering to take my dad's place and go to the picnic. But I wasn't sure I could stomach playing the perfect, straight-A daughter and making small talk with my mom's teacher friends. They were nice enough, but I was tired and . . . edgy.

I figured Dad could handle a few hours of hot dogs and small talk.

Mom came to my door and poked her head in. "We're leaving now."

"Okay."

"You'll check on her, right? I left dinner for both of you. Try to get her to eat."

"Sure."

Mom came over and hugged me. "Sorry. I forgot to say how much I missed you."

At least she realized it.

"Did you have fun with your dad?"

I nodded, and she turned to leave. "Okay, well, call if . . . if you need anything."

"I will."

"Every hour, right? You won't forget? We can't get complacent, you know."

"I *know*."

She smiled but pushed the door open as she left, the gesture obvious, meant to remind me of Darby just down the hall. I stalled in my room until I heard the front door close.

It was always awkward figuring out exactly what to say to Darby. I decided to pop my head in to let her know I was home, hoping that would be "normal" enough. If babysitting your older sister could ever be considered in the realm of normal.

The door was ajar, and I pushed it open a little more.

I put on my cheery voice. "Hey, I'm home."

Instantly I regretted my decision. She was curled up on her bed asleep on top of her books. My words startled her awake.

She gave a frustrated sigh and shoved a book. "What time is it?" she asked.

I leaned on her door. "It's one. Mom and Dad left for the picnic. Did you have lunch yet?"

Darby shook her head. "I'm not hungry. I need to finish studying."

I tried to read her expression. She seemed upset, but I wasn't sure why. *Is it serious? Or is it nothing?* "Okay, well, let me know if you change your mind." I closed the door slowly, watching her open a book.

Always the same two questions but never an answer.

CHAPTER 2

"You're avoiding me," Tess said as I climbed into her Jeep Monday morning.

"I am not."

Tess gave me her "Do you think I'm an idiot?" look.

I spent all day Sunday getting ready for this moment, but now I couldn't get my tongue to work.

Step 1: Admit that I am powerless over my lying. My life, really. *Done.*

Step 2: Believe that God could restore me to sanity. *Yes.*

Step 3: Turn my life over to God. *I think?*

Step 4: Make a moral inventory. *Yes.*

I had an exhaustive and embarrassing list of accumulated lies, all told to protect myself. And my family. Making the list was one thing. It was Step 5 that seemed impossible: Admit to God, myself, and another human being the exact nature of my wrongs.

Tess was the obvious person to tell. But I couldn't do it.

"What is it?" Tess demanded.

"Nothing. A fight. Todd and I had a fight."

Yvie and Sophie were waiting in the parking lot for us when we pulled in. Yvie was tall, leggy, and the object of every guy's desire. Sophie was a more exotic beauty. The four of us had been friends since middle school. Tess and I were the closest, though, so when they approached, I knew that another day would go by with no confession.

"What's going on?" Sophie asked.

Tess jabbed her thumb at me. "Mallory and Todd had a fight."

Yvie was leaning on the Jeep, texting. "Well, he'd better show up for homecoming. You swore on your computer."

Sophie held her hand to her heart. "The bloom of romance is fading." Leave it to Sophie to be dramatic.

"It's just a fight. Can we go inside now?"

Tess gave me another one of her looks.

I could only avoid dealing with Todd for so long.

But it wasn't Tess or the Twelve Steps that was on my mind as I sat through trig. I stared at the back of Liam Crawford's head—an actual guy with bones and skin and everything.

Liam Crawford. He was bent over his paper writing something, his brown curls a mop on his head. In the six weeks he had been at North County, Liam and I had exchanged maybe a dozen words. We ran in different crowds. I was a varsity cheerleader, and while I wasn't one of the über-popular like Yvie or Sophie, Tess and I had carved out our own happy niche. We were near enough to the in-crowd never to lack an invitation to a party but far enough away from the center not to be under constant pressure.

It was a place where I could breathe. And Todd was a part of that. Todd was my ready excuse for anything I didn't want to have to explain. Any time I just wanted an out.

As much as I wanted to get rid of him, I wasn't sure what a life without Todd would even look like.

"Liam," Mr. Petrini called out. Liam stood up and walked toward the teacher's desk, and they had a brief conversation that I couldn't hear.

Mr. Petrini looked up and said, "Who has time to walk Mr. Crawford over to the Tech Center and show him where the testing room is?"

My hand shot up in the air so quickly I knocked my book to the floor.

Oh. My. God.

Mr. Petrini smirked. "Thanks, Mallory. You two can be excused."

I shoved my book into my backpack and avoided Tess's eyes. Liam took his backpack, slung it over his shoulder, and waited at the door. Everyone was focused on their work. Mr. Petrini went back to his computer. But I still felt as if everyone was watching me walk toward Liam. As if I needed dramatic background music.

I mean, I knew I had been watching Liam, but this? This was not in the plan.

Liam grinned when I reached him and held the door open for me.

When the door closed and it was just us and a long, empty hallway, he said, "Mallory. That's a pretty name."

"Thanks."

It was quiet for a moment.

I knew I should ask a question. Why wouldn't my brain work?

"So, am I your good deed for the day?" he asked.

"Do you think this counts?"

"Absolutely." He smiled. "All I know about you is that you're a cheerleader, right? I saw you at the pep rally last week."

He noticed me. That was *interesting*. "Yep. I'm a cheerleader. That's about it."

"I doubt that's all there is to know about you."

"Maybe. Maybe not. But we've only got five more minutes before you're safely delivered to the testing room. Why do you have to go, anyway?"

"It's something with my records. They have to sort out my credits so I can graduate on time, and that means I have to take another placement test."

"Sounds fun." I found myself smiling back at him. It was easier than I thought it would be. Talking to him. I had imagined it. But I usually imagined it as a disaster.

I led him out a back door so that we could cross the field to the Tech Center.

"Wow. Wish we could have class out here today."

I didn't know what to say to that so I waited, and sure enough, he jumped back in. He was a lot better at this than I was. "Tell me something about yourself besides cheerleading."

I looked at the ground. That should be an easy question. A really easy one. But my thoughts flitted to everything I *didn't* want to say. We got all the way to the testing-room door and still I had nothing.

Liam leaned against the wall and shoved his hands into his pockets. He was taller than me by maybe four inches. He looked like he'd be willing to wait forever.

"Maybe next time," I said. "You should go."

Liam gave me a look I couldn't read, then opened the door. "Promise?"

"Sure."

He went inside, and I let out a breath I didn't even know I had been holding.

I hurried back toward school, toward Tess, feeling disoriented. What just happened? On the surface it looked so simple and basic. But I knew it wasn't. It was like something—I wasn't sure what yet—had opened before me.

The question was, What was I going to do about it?

I found Tess already eating in the cafeteria. I passed through the salad line and went to sit with her.

"What was that?" she asked.

"What was what?"

"The new dude. Since when are you Miss Volunteerism?"

"Just doing my good deed for the day." I shoved food into my mouth, enjoying the fact that I had shocked Tess.

That wasn't an easy thing to do.

Darby was sitting at the kitchen table when I got home, her college textbooks scattered around and her laptop casting a bluish glow on her face.

I flipped on the kitchen light, making her squint.

"You'll ruin your eyes!" I said in my best Mom impersonation.

Darby rolled hers in response. "I didn't realize it had gotten so dark in here."

I yanked open the fridge and rummaged around until I found a drinkable yogurt. I peeled back the lid and sat down at the table.

"What'cha doin'?" I asked.

Darby stared at the computer as her finger moved on the mouse pad. "I'm just stuck. It's an essay for English."

"Ohhh." I drank the rest of my yogurt. "Have you been sitting here all day?"

Darby looked at the clock above the back door and smirked. "I guess I have." She stretched her arms and closed the laptop. "Maybe a break would be good. Want to go for a walk?"

I glanced at the clock. I had exactly an hour before Tess would be in the driveway to pick me up for the game. I wanted to go upstairs and have time to figure everything out. But Mom's guilt-laden voice in my head was too loud to ignore.

"Sure. Not too far, though. Let me go tell Dad I'm home."

She closed down her laptop and then gave me a smile.

I went to the basement and found Dad already packing up his stuff.

"Your mom said she'd be back before you have to leave for the game. I've got to get out of here. I'm late for an appointment."

"I'm sorry. I got back as quick as I could."

He kissed me on the head. "No problem. I don't think she ate dinner yet. Your mom will ask."

We came back upstairs, and after a quick good-bye to Darby, he left.

I followed Darby out through the back doorway and through the gate. She picked the trail today. The trail meant that she was in a melancholy mood and didn't really want to run into neighbors or have to smile at people walking their dogs.

We made our way through the woods until we got to the trail. The leaves were just starting to change. I watched Darby as she looked around and took it all in. I wondered, as

I always did, what she was really thinking. I wasn't allowed to ask. With Darby, there were so many rules. What I could say, what I couldn't say—all from Mom and all under the guise of Darby's therapy. Like I could make or break Darby's recovery with every word I said. It was easier just to not say much of anything.

When we turned around to head back home, Darby broke her silence.

"Sorry. I'm not feeling very chatty today." She stepped over a small log and smiled back at me.

"That's okay. Me neither."

"How's school?"

"Fine."

"Cheerleading?"

"Fine."

"You're going to give me the standard answers, huh?"

I shrugged. Even though Darby was older than me and there were small signs that she was getting better, I still had to feel my way through every conversation, always keep up the smile.

She didn't ask anything else, and by the time we reached home, I was nervous about being ready in time. After Darby was settled back in front of the computer, I took a quick shower and then went to my room to change.

Todd was everywhere I looked. The room was covered with pictures of Todd, and Todd and me.

I walked over to my dresser and picked up the beach one, cheek to cheek (not an easy thing to do with Photoshop btw) with happy smiles on our faces. I felt . . . sad. I opened my little moleskin notebook where I tucked away the Twelve Step program and looked at the steps again. That stupid

Step 5. How would I ever be able to confess my pathetic lies to another person?

Todd wasn't exactly an alcohol addiction, but my life had certainly become unmanageable, and I *definitely* needed help. I could admit that. But did taking back my life really mean I had to tell everyone the truth about Todd?

Nah. I just needed to be free of him. Why confess when we could just break up?

So even though I was already running late, I opened my closet and pulled out an empty plastic container and set it on my desk. I told myself I had to get rid of him—for real this time. And that meant total deletion.

Making up Todd wasn't premeditated. It was like one of those little white lies that you throw out there, but it sticks with you for so long that it grows legs and starts running your life. For all the help Todd gave me, he was a constant reminder that I was a total fake.

Before, there had always been just the four of us: Tess, Yvie, Sophie, and me. We were only freshmen when Yvie told us at a sleepover one night that she had slept with her boyfriend, Mark. We were stunned. Yvie said that getting it over with would make high school less stressful. I don't think any of us actually believed her; but as time passed, Sophie and then even Tess had come back with tales of their journeys out of virginity, leaving just me. Yes, there was pressure. I'd only gone on a handful of dates, but I'd still get the "Did you do it?" stare from at least one of them. I felt as if I had been left behind in some way.

Then last Christmas when things had gone nuts with Darby and I couldn't tell anyone what was happening, I'd made up a story about how my grandmother was sick and we had to keep going out of town to see her. When that raised questions, I'd made up Todd, who conveniently lived next door to my grandmother. And since none of my friends would ever know that I hadn't slept with him, I'd just gone back and told them I had.

Pretending I had done it seemed way easier than admitting that I didn't want to have sex. Which I didn't. Maybe I had watched too many Disney movies growing up, or maybe it was because of everything Darby went through, but I kind of wanted the whole fairy-tale romance—not some quickie, get-it-over-with thing that I had to hold my breath and get through.

Inventing Todd hadn't been all that hard. Working with my dad had made me a whiz at Photoshop. One fake online profile and some great pictures were all it took. Nobody asked too many questions, and I no longer felt like some outcast. Ironically, it did take off a lot of pressure.

But then I couldn't seem to get rid of him.

I tried. I really did. But every time I would break up with fake Todd, I would start getting crazy nervous about the whole dating scene. With my mom and Darby, I didn't have much freedom to go anywhere besides cheerleading, anyway. Then there was the fact that a real guy could assume I'd sleep with him, too. It felt as if the whole school was more experienced than I was. And real relationships seemed full of all sorts of drama that I couldn't afford. Todd was easier; he was completely controllable.

I picked up the beach picture and put it in the box and then worked my way around the room, quickly untaping each and every picture of Todd and stacking them all in the box. There was an impressive amount of pictures. I stared at the pile for a while. I had broken up with Todd before, but I never went this far, putting our pretend world away in a box. It was a big step.

I reached behind the mirror and slid out the notebook that was wedged behind a support bar. The Todd notebook. Every part of Todd's life was documented in here. Where he was born, the names of his family members, trips he'd been on, and even all of his identifying characteristics. He's got a cute little mole on his right jawline. I smiled, flipping through the book, remembering. . . .

I shook my head. *Stop it! Enough with the delusion already.* I slapped the notebook closed and then slid it underneath all the pictures at the bottom of the box and snapped on the lid. For extra measure I took a roll of masking tape and wound it around the box over and over. I tore off the end of the masking tape and patted it down. That oughta do it.

Todd was gone.

Dead, gone, and buried.

Tess honked a second time before I made it out to the car and slumped into the passenger seat. She held out her phone to me.

"I find out on the Internet?"

"Oh. That."

"Yes, that. I should not be finding out at the same exact time as the rest of the world."

"Sorry."

Tess backed out of the driveway. "Spill it."

Another opportunity to confess handed to me.

"He said he needed space."

And another opportunity missed.

"Space? Like a three-hour drive isn't enough space? Whatever. He's dead weight, Mal."

"It's probably for the best, right?"

"Duh. I've been saying that the whole time. This doesn't have anything to do with Liam, does it?"

"Liam?" I kept the smile from spreading across my face at his name, but Tess didn't need confirmation.

"It's about time. Is he coming to the game?"

"No idea."

"Liam does have one glaring character flaw."

"What?"

"His association with Alex Yeager. Of course, that also means he'll be at the party tonight."

"A party?" These after-game parties were a regular part of football season, even on school nights; but it would mean a call to my mom and—

"Mal. You're free. I think that's cause for serious celebration. What's wrong? Cheerleaders are supposed to be happy. You're not going to be all moody tonight, are you?"

"I just had a breakup. Let me mourn."

"No. No mourning allowed. And don't even think about getting back together with him."

"I'm not." I held up my hands as if I were being arrested or something.

"Yes, you are. I can see it in your weepy eyes."

"My eyes are not weepy." I shrugged one shoulder. "It's just . . ."

"I knew it! Mallory. We're juniors. You can't waste the

best years of your life with some long-distance guy who doesn't even have the time to visit."

"The best years of my life?"

"Whatever. I know you're sad and *wah-wah-wah* and all of that, but this is, like, the greatest news ever."

Tess's cell rang and she answered it, giving me a moment to catch my breath. I congratulated myself on not spilling the depth of my crush on Liam. It was way too early to let Tess in on that one. I needed to get through the fake grieving process first. Besides, Tess would throw herself into planning and plotting a myriad of ways to "Get Mallory and Liam in the same space." Too soon for that much attention. But if Liam happened to be at the party, maybe another casual conversation could keep things going in the right direction.

"Fine. Fine. FINE!" Tess snapped her phone shut and squeezed the steering wheel.

"Tess?"

She bit her lip.

"Your mom?"

"Always," she said.

"You can stay at my house tonight." I silently hoped that things would be quiet and normal at my house.

Tess nodded, staring ahead. I watched her, knowing that by the time we got to school, Tess would be back and the phone conversation would be forgotten, at least for the game and the party. I twisted the small ring on my right hand upside down so that the green stone was underneath. Tess and I bought the matching rings years ago. It would help me remember to check in with her later that night, when no one else was around. It would be the only time I'd get her to talk about it, anyway.

True to form, when we pulled into the parking lot, Tess bounced out of the Jeep and unzipped the back for our bags.

She grinned. "You ready?"

"Ready."

CHAPTER 3

The trouble with lying is that once you start, you have to lie all the time. You tell lies to cover up your lies. And even if I wanted to, I couldn't quit lying completely because there were questions to be answered.

From Yvie: "Are you really broken up or are you guys just fighting?"

"Nope. For real this time. It's over," I told her.

From Sophie: "But you said he was coming to home-coming this year!"

Yeah, that was the other major problem solved by the breakup. Adorable Liam might have given me the gumption to get rid of Todd, but the looming "I swear on my iMac" promise I'd made to bring Todd to homecoming this year was a nice incentive.

Tess had my back, though, as always. "The name Todd is off-limits." Tess drew her hand across her throat. "No more." She linked her arm with mine to head to the locker room, waving good-bye to Yvie and Sophie, neither of whom could ever be convinced to join us on the squad.

Tess squeezed my arm. "It's going to be a great year for you."

I squeezed back. And hoped she was right.

We cheered and danced underneath the glaring lights on the field, trying to whip the crowd into a frenzy. We were winning the game, barely, and I was having more fun than I'd ever thought possible. I was free. A fresh start was exactly what I needed. During a time-out, I walked to the fence line, where our bags and pom-poms made a purple-and-white line. I grabbed my water bottle and squirted some water into my mouth.

Then I stood up and came face-to-face with Liam. Alex was there, too, but he was just a fuzzy outline on the periphery.

"Hey, Mallory," Liam said. *He's here. He sought me out.*

I tried to swallow the water in my mouth and smile at the same time, which didn't work at all. Liam cocked his head and gave me a funny look just as I ran out of breath. I gasped some air, sucked water into my throat, and began coughing uncontrollably.

I bent over to spare myself from the humiliation and felt someone clapping me on my back. I coughed and coughed and coughed. *Will it never end?*

"Are you okay? Do you want some water?" It was Tess. She was bent down with one hand hitting my back. I grabbed her other hand and pulled her closer.

"Are they still watching?" I choked out between coughs.

"Yep."

I stayed down until I had complete control of my breathing and furiously wiped at my eyes, which were leaking like faucets. I could only hope my face wasn't bright red.

I stood up and drank a little more water—carefully this time.

Alex was definitely snickering, but I couldn't read Liam's face. Was that concern?

"You all right?" Liam asked.

I tried desperately to think of something witty to say, but all that came out of my mouth was "Yeah."

That was the best I could do?

"We have to get back. We'll see you guys tonight," Tess said. She pulled me out onto the track, where Tara, the squad captain, was setting up for another dance number.

"You are totally holding out on me. I can't believe you." Tess turned and waved at the crowds on the bleachers.

"What?" I took my place beside her. I could see Sam messing with the music by the fence line.

"I've never seen you look at a guy like that. *Ever.*"

The music started, loud and pulsating, saving me from responding to Tess. I dropped my head and arms into position. Was I that obvious? And if I was, how did I ever get away with Todd?

Tess mercifully waited until we were back in her car on the way to Alex's party before grilling me.

"And you kept that from me *why*?"

I shrugged.

"Mallory."

"What? There isn't anything to tell. He's cute. You said the same thing the day he started school, remember?"

"Yeah, but you were not looking at him like 'Oh, he's cute.' You were more like 'Wow, I want you.'"

"I was not."

Tess just stared at me.

"Fine. You win. But we're not going to do anything about it, okay?"

"I'm not going to. But you are. You've got five weeks until homecoming; and you, my friend, are going with Liam."

I sat back against the seat. "I don't know if I'm ready."

Tess was quiet for several minutes before she answered. "You've been ready for a long time."

Tess and I caught up with Sophie and Yvie on the back porch, where the party was already in full swing. It was a perfect Indian summer night. Alex lived out of town a little bit; and where the manicured yard ended, a thick forest began. Tess didn't say anything about Liam to the other girls, but when he came out the back door and walked onto the lawn below us, she bumped my shoulder and jutted her chin toward him.

"He and Alex really hit it off, didn't they?" Tess said.

I nodded, watching Liam talk and laugh in a circle of guys. He looked up and saw me on the porch—I was sure of it—but then he turned away. No smile. No wave.

What happened? "Did you see that?" I asked Tess.

Tess nodded.

All of a sudden I felt like an idiot. Not only had Liam ignored me, but he'd shifted completely away from me. Like he didn't even want to look at me.

"Did you say anything to him?" Tess asked.

"No." I watched him talk and laugh with the guys, and when I couldn't take it anymore, I turned my back.

"You should go talk to him," Tess said.

"Why bother?"

"Take a risk. It might be worth it."

Even with Todd packed up in that little box in my closet, I felt incredibly guilty. The lies were going to suffocate me before I could get out from under them. And I hated that I had lied to Tess for so long. She probably would've understood.

I was a liar and a lousy friend. So I wasn't exactly in any kind of mood to find out what went sour during the game.

Tess stared out into the yard, too, her eyes wide and still, looking past all the kids. I bumped her shoulder.

"Wanna talk about it?" I asked.

Tess shook her head, breaking out of the gaze, and gave me a half smile. "Later," she said. "Right now, we're both going down there." She pointed into the yard and grabbed my elbow, maneuvering us through the crowd, down the stairs, and onto the lawn.

"Did you check out the peanut site?" Tess asked.

We were trying to organize a fund-raiser to get new uniforms for the team. It was Tess's way of making a bid for team captain when we became seniors and my way of helping her do it.

"I hate selling things. And peanuts remind me of Girl Scouts. Not a fun memory."

"I know, but the profits are good and . . ." She stopped. "He's definitely ignoring you. Let's crash the circle," she whispered.

We walked over, and Alex went right for Tess.

"Tessie," Alex said.

"Hey." Tess gave me a look that let me know that she would only tolerate Alex for my sake. She had dated Alex for over a year, but they broke up halfway through sophomore year. She said she lost interest, but I knew there was more to the story. Everyone has their secrets.

Alex put his arm around her shoulder, and she deftly slipped it right back off. He seemed a little drunk. "C'mon, Tessie."

"Would you excuse us?" she said to Liam, and then dragged Alex away from us, closer to the tree line. I couldn't hear her, but she was pointing her finger at him. Not a good sign.

Liam looked at Tess and Alex, then slowly looked back toward me.

"So, you and Tess. Been friends a long time?" His voice didn't hold the same warm feel as it had earlier. It was polite. But cold.

"Since third grade." I tried to steady my nerves. "Where did you live before this?" It was the question I should have asked when we first spoke at school.

"Everywhere. My dad's in the military, so every two years, new school, new friends, new everything."

"That sucks."

He shook his head. "Just the way it is." He was quiet for what seemed like forever, and I couldn't come up with another question. I realized that both Tess and Alex were gone at the same time Liam finally spoke up. "So, I hear you have a boyfriend."

Oh.

"No. Where'd you hear that?" I asked.

"Actually, everywhere." He held up his phone. "Multiple texts. Funny how much information is offered when you ask about a girl."

My heart sank. "You shouldn't believe everything you hear. We broke up. A while ago."

Liam's entire posture and expression changed, melting from guarded distance to that soft warmth I'd felt from him before. "Mallory. I . . . I didn't . . . I'm sorry. I should have just asked you myself."

"I have to go find Tess." I slipped into the crowd, ignoring his protests. Todd was still following me everywhere. I just wanted to find Tess and get out of here.

I did a quick sweep of the backyard from the porch and then walked through the downstairs portion of the house, and still there was no sign of Tess.

I spotted Yvie sitting on a couch in the basement, and from across the room I mouthed *Tess?* and held out my hands. Yvie shook her head and returned her attention to J.C., her current flame, and all of her admirers. She looked like a queen holding court.

I decided to try upstairs and soon found a locked bathroom door.

I knocked. "Tess, are you in there?"

There was no answer. I turned away to keep looking, then heard the lock click on the door. I opened it. "Tess?"

Tess slid down the far wall and put her head on her knees, her shoulders moving in silent sobs.

"Oh, Tessie."

I pulled the door closed and locked it before squeezing in beside her and the tub.

"What'd he do?"

Tess lifted her head and swiped at the tears running down her face. Tess hardly ever cried, so seeing the distraught look on her face shook me a little. I was the emotional one. She was the rock. It was how our relationship usually worked.

"What happened?" I urged.

"It's over."

"But . . . it's been over."

"I know. I mean, I know that. I just thought he'd quit being such a jerk someday. That he'd realize he'd lost me. That he'd for once use his brain to make a decision."

I didn't know what to say. She had dumped him, and he had been trying to get her back—but she was crying because he didn't succeed?

"Tess, I'm sorry, but I'm lost here. Help me out."

She leaned her head back against the wall and wrapped her arms around her knees. "I didn't realize, until like ten minutes ago, how over it really was. He's not going to change." She wiped at her face again. "So now we both need dates for homecoming."

I wasn't going to let her switch the subject that easily. "What did he do?"

"He slept with Cammie Herst. And it shouldn't bother me. It shouldn't matter what he does with himself any-more. . . ."

But obviously it did. I leaned my head against hers and tried to think of something brilliant and profound to say. But nothing came. Other than some random thoughts of causing bodily harm to Alex, I didn't know how to make any of it better.

On the way home, Tess shut down talk of Alex and turned the subject back to the fund-raiser. It wasn't until we walked into my room that she stopped debating profit margins. She dropped her bag and did a slow three-sixty in the center of my room.

"What happened in here?"

The walls did look pretty blank without Todd anywhere.

She looked at me. "So you really did it this time."

I glanced around, still not used to the bareness myself. "Yeah."

She threw her arms around me and squeezed. "I'm so proud of you. Did you find out why Liam was being a jerk?"

"Yeah."

"And . . ."

"Rumors. Apparently he was offered a great deal of info about me."

"You told him you don't have a boyfriend, right?"

"Yeah. But it doesn't matter."

Tess pushed me. "Yes, it does! One, you talked to him. And two, you talked to him after breaking up with Todd. We should shoot off fireworks or something."

"Speaking of fireworks. Your mom?" I twisted the ring on my finger.

Tess's grin slid from her face, and her eyes darkened. "There's nothing new to tell you. Just the same story on continuous replay. She makes me feel like the psycho. And my sister? If I were older, I'd take Ashley and leave."

"I thought your mom was going to that counselor."

Tess let out a hard laugh. "Yeah, that lasted one session. A record for her, though." Tess changed into a T-shirt and cotton pants.

"Did you keep anything?" she asked, switching gears.

"Why bother?"

"Oh, I don't know. It's just so weird to see your room like this." She pulled a notebook from her backpack and then sat cross-legged on the bed. "Okay. We need to plan the best fund-raiser ever."

Tess didn't want to think about her mom. And I wasn't about to make her.

So I went with it.

CHAPTER 4

Tess drove me to school, and we rode in mutual silence. Neither of us were "morning people," so we had an ongoing pact to give each other space to get coherent before speaking. It usually worked pretty well, but Tess had been woken up by a cell phone call from her mother and was fuming. We swung by her house so that she could check on Ashley. Tess came out quickly, but I could tell that she was still really upset.

So I broke the pact.

"Was Ashley okay?"

Tess kept her eyes on the road. "She's fine. But she didn't have any lunch money, clean clothes, or anything to eat for breakfast. I gave her extra so she could eat at school."

"And your mom?"

Tess scowled. "Passed out again. I never spoke to her."

Tess pulled into the parking lot and jammed the Jeep into park. But as soon as she stood up and closed the door, she seemed to shake off the reality of what was going on at home and put a smile on her face.

I was totally impressed every time.

We went inside together, and even though I was panicky about seeing Liam, Tess standing beside me made everything in my life feel desperately small and unimportant.

Tess's mom had always been unpredictable and irresponsible. But I could tell that something had shifted for the worse inside her house.

Tess was always there for me. She never made me feel as if my problems were small. And yet here was a chance for me to be there for her, and I didn't know what to do. It was a monster-sized problem with no easy solution.

It's funny, though, how high school can suck you in. As soon as we sat down in homeroom, it was like cheerleading and fund-raisers and homecoming became über-important. Tess and I had come up with a fund-raising plan. It was pretty ambitious, but Tess thought we could pull it off. She reasoned that not many people really care about new uniforms for cheerleaders, so we had to do something that would make people interested. She wanted to do a dual fund-raiser for the local domestic violence shelter and our uniforms. Her grand plan was to hold a toy drive to collect gently used toys for the day care center in the shelter, and during the toy drive we would do a "Pictures with Santa" for the kids. Most of the money from the pictures would go toward the uniforms. Everybody would win.

There were about a million things we had to work out if we were going to pull it off before Christmas; plus we were going to need a whole lot of help. Help that Tess was quite capable of rallying.

And then there was Liam. I didn't have any classes with him on A Day, but I had two on B Day. Trig and English. So since it was A Day, that meant I could only see him in the hallways and at lunch.

I wanted to see him—and *didn't* want to see him—both at the same time.

What I wasn't prepared for was seeing him in a close conversation with Lexi Taylor.

Lexi was one of those good-girl quiet types who I never really took much notice of—until I saw her flirting with

Liam. I watched the whole exchange, and even though most people would have seen it as some casual hallway convo, I knew I was in trouble.

Is Liam dating Lexi? How do I not know this? I felt way more upset about it than was reasonable.

Fortunately, Lexi was in my PE class. It would be better to find out the truth.

"Hey, Lexi. Want to be my partner?" I asked after I was changed and standing in the archery field. Lexi looked surprised, as did Katie, another cheerleader and my usual partner.

"Sure." She picked up one of the targets. "Wanna get the arrows?"

After we got the target set up and measured our distance, we stood next to each other, taking turns trying to hit the bull's-eye.

"I saw you talking to the new guy this morning—Liam, isn't it?"

"Yeah." She let an arrow fly, but it stuck in the ground in front of the target. "Shoot."

I set up my shot. "Do you know him?"

"Yeah."

I rolled my eyes. *Does she not know how to elaborate?* "How did you meet him?"

"He goes to my church."

Finally something more than a one-word answer. Church. That was practically the only thing I knew about Lexi. She was a church kid.

She fell quiet again as we took turns shooting and gathering the arrows. Lexi was as bad at archery as she was at having this conversation.

I decided to keep trying. "So, are you and Liam . . . friends?"

"Yeah. You could say that." Her arrow flew and hit right outside the center. She squealed, then handed me the bow. "Why are you so interested in Liam?"

"No reason."

"He's not really your type, you know."

"What is that supposed to mean?" How could she presume to know my type? *I* didn't even know my type. I let the arrow fly, sending it straight into the center.

She wasn't intimidated. She held up a finger on her right hand, and for a split second I thought that Lexi, Miss Goody Two-Shoes herself, was flipping me off. "He's a Christian. He noticed my promise ring this morning." She pointed to a ring on her right hand. "That's why we were talking."

"So? Why do you think you know what my type is, anyway?" I shoved the bow toward her, and she took it.

She jammed it into the ground. "I'm not stupid. Just because I'm quiet doesn't mean that I don't know what goes on at this school."

I shifted but kept staring at her, still unsure exactly what she was getting at.

She picked up another arrow. "All I mean is that you're popular, and, well, he's just not that type of guy."

Now she looked uncomfortable.

"So because I'm popular, he wouldn't be interested in me? Is that what you're saying?"

"No. It's more than that."

"Then what is it?"

"You wouldn't understand."

I will not kill Lexi. I will not kill Lexi. "You think Liam is too good for someone like me?"

Lexi's eyes widened. "No, that's not what I'm saying."

"Then what are you saying?"

Lexi stared, her eyes glassy. "I'm sorry . . . I just . . ." She dropped the bow on the ground and ran back toward the gym.

I stood there with a handful of arrows feeling hurt, confused, and a little guilty.

I filled in Tess on my Lexi encounter at lunchtime.

"Okay, now that's weird."

"Yeah, but she obviously didn't tell me everything. Do you think he'll only date girls like Lexi or what?"

"I don't know. Maybe you should ask him."

I looked over at where Liam was sitting with some guys at a table by the windows. It was one thing to try to get info from Lexi, but talking to Liam again was a whole other proposition.

"Or just ask him out and get it over with. Mallory, you're stressing over nothing. There are plenty of other guys who would go out with you."

But I didn't want to go out with plenty of other guys. And I couldn't even explain why I liked Liam. There was just something totally different about him. I was drawn to him. I loved the way he tapped out a rhythm on his jeans with his pencil when he was thinking hard in class. I loved how when he smiled, it made me want to smile, too. It had been so easy to stick with Todd before, because while I had found a few guys in my school cute and nice, I never really cared enough to do anything about it.

Liam changed all that, and I had no plausible explanation for it.

Tess threw her straw wrapper at me. "Snap out of it, girl. Just do it. What do you have to lose?"

"My dignity."

Tess laughed. "Dignity is overrated. And if you don't want him dating Lexi Do-Gooder by next weekend, you'd better do something. Because somehow, he doesn't seem like the kind of guy to date around."

And Tess was totally right. As usual. But I couldn't bring myself to do anything except stare at him from across crowded hallways. Which really wasn't very useful.

I dragged myself to cheerleading practice and tried to focus on Tess's fund-raising event. She stood in front of the entire JV and varsity squad and went through her plan. I knew about it and was still impressed. The coaches asked most of the questions, but at the end they gave her the go-ahead to put together a committee to pull it off. Everyone split up to practice, and she came bouncing over to me.

"I can't believe it. So you'll help me, of course, but who else should we recruit?" Tess turned and looked out across the gym. Everyone was inside because of the rain. "Maybe Olivia. She's like a math whiz. That would be helpful," she said.

"Should we ask any of the seniors?"

"I was thinking no, because what do they care if we get new uniforms for next year? They'll be gone. The juniors will work harder, don't you think?"

I agreed. It was also the juniors who would get to vote for team captain. Smart girl.

By the end of practice we had a committee, and I realized that Tess's project was going to take a huge chunk of time. I was put in charge of trying to find a building where we could collect the toys and do the pictures, for free, during the first part of November.

I decided to enlist Darby's help for two reasons. One: Mom's rules included finding ways to keep her involved with the family (as long as it wasn't stressful). And two: she had a car—a major advantage.

After I told Dad he was relieved of his Darby-sitting duties that night, I found Darby on the back porch with her laptop, asleep.

"Darby?"

She stirred, opened one eye, then sat up slowly. "I fell asleep." She looked up at me. "How long did I sleep?"

"No idea. I just got back."

"I hate these meds. Hate them. I was actually getting that stupid essay done and then I fall asleep."

She didn't seem to be in a very good mood, so favor asking was risky.

She opened her laptop and then growled, "Well, at least it's saved. Mom's got some teacher meeting thing tonight."

"Well, I was going to see if you wanted to help me with something."

She looked up. "Like what?"

I filled her in on the fund-raiser and my need to be driven around town to beg for space.

"Sure." Darby gathered up her laptop and papers. "Let's go."

After we grabbed dinner at the Sub Shop, we drove around town looking for buildings that were vacant and for lease. A lot of them were too small; but we gathered names, addresses, and phone numbers for the ones that seemed large enough. In the end there were only about five possibilities.

"Why don't you let me call around?" Darby asked when we got home.

"Oh, I can do it; it's fine. This was a huge help."

"Well, lots of these are businesses, and they're going to be closed by the time you get back from practice. I don't mind."

I hesitated, weighing whether the task was too much pressure or the right kind of involvement. I wasn't sure, but I needed the help, so I handed her the list. "If you're willing, I'm game." I also gave her the info that Tess had typed up about the project.

"I think this is great. When I was in school, all the cheerleaders did was try to look sexier."

"Not Tess."

"I'll call around and see what I can find out. You don't mind me stepping in?"

"No way. I'm thrilled. Ecstatic. Thanks, Darby."

She smiled sadly. Her dark moods were pretty standard fare, but I still wondered what was on her mind. Darby had been through so much that it could be any one of a dozen things nagging at her. I felt a little guilty, but Darby wouldn't have offered to help if she wasn't willing. That's what I'd tell Mom when she asked.

I called Tess to let her know that Darby was going to work on securing the building.

"I'm picking you up then."

"Why?"

"'Cause if Darby's doing your job, then you can help with mine."

I didn't argue. Mom was on her way home by that point, so I wouldn't get in trouble for leaving Darby. I changed and waited by the front door. Tess pulled up in her Jeep.

"Did you ask your dad yet?"

"Not yet. He left as soon as I got home."

She wanted me to borrow one of my dad's digital cameras for the pictures to save money. He had all the equipment—the cameras, the computers, the printers—but talking Dad into letting a bunch of cheerleaders use them was not something I was eager to do. I knew how to use the equipment, but I was no expert. My personal plan was to convince Dad to come and help us that day instead of me being responsible for thousands of dollars' worth of equipment. I wasn't comfortable with that kind of responsibility.

"But he'll say yes, right?"

"Probably."

That satisfied her.

Tess drove to Hope House, the local domestic violence shelter. She parked, and I followed her inside the building, which was basically a large, two-story house. A heavy-set woman with short red hair came out of a small office next to the entrance.

"Tessie! I haven't seen you in ages." The woman squashed Tess into a hug. "What brings you by?"

"I have an idea that might help us both," Tess said. "This is my friend Mallory. Mallory, this is Tammy."

"Come on into my closet here and we can talk. Your friend can come, too."

I looked at the tiny office, barely big enough for its owner much less two teenagers. "I'll wait out here."

Tess settled into a chair to give Tammy the pitch while I leaned on a wall in the hallway. I looked around at the simple home. A stairwell led upstairs, and the hallway I was standing in led back to a kitchen that was full of different voices. A small sitting room was across from me. It was shabby but clean, with couches and some bookshelves and tables.

Tess had stayed here for more than a year when we were in fifth grade. I remembered it well.

Looking around, it wasn't hard to imagine Tess living there. I actually wished there were a place for her to go now. A safe place for kids to go when their moms were too drunk to take care of them. I wondered if Tammy could help Tess, if Tess was willing to ask.

Tess came out of the office, followed by Tammy, who was wiping her eyes.

"Thank you, Tess. You know how much it will mean to the kids here."

"Well, we're hoping to get enough toys to give some for Christmas, too, but we'll have to see."

Tammy grabbed Tess into another hug. "You're an angel. Truly. Is your family doing okay? Your mom?"

Tess waved her hand. "Everything's great. You don't mind if we take a look at what kind of stuff you already have?"

"Nope, go on down. They closed up already."

Tess gestured for me to follow her to a set of stairs that

led down to the day care center in the basement. It was a little dark, but some light came in from the sliding door in the back. Outside, I could see playground equipment. Tess flipped on the lights and started walking around the room with a notepad, writing down things.

"What do you want me to do?" I asked.

"Can you start on that side? Just write down what they have and what's missing pieces and all that. I think it'll help when we go through the stuff we get."

She tore off paper for me, and we worked our way around the room. There were toys, but not many. And most of them were missing parts: wood puzzles that had only half their pieces, plastic dollhouses with only a few pieces of furniture. It was sad.

It didn't take us very long, and after a quick look at the playground, we were back in her Jeep.

"Hey, Tess."

"Hmmm?"

"How come you didn't tell Tammy? About your mom. I mean, maybe she could help."

"She can't," Tess said. "And if I tell her, she'll have to call social services, and that'll land us both in foster care. And I'm not going into foster care, or letting them take Ashley. They'd have to kill me first."

Tess parked the car in my driveway and leaned back in her seat.

"I only have to make it eighteen more months, and I can become Ashley's legal guardian."

"But what about college and all of that?"

"It'll just take me longer. Believe me, it's better this way. I can deal with my mom. I have been, anyway. Tell Darby thanks for me."

"No problem." I left the car and watched her pull out and drive off waving. I trudged back into the house, feeling helpless.

Mom was at the sink washing dishes. I looked at her for signs that she might be angry with me for being so busy this week, but she seemed fairly content.

"There you are. Did you eat?"

"Yeah."

She dried her hands on a towel. "What's wrong?"

I looked at her, all normal and motherly, and felt this rush of gratitude. I gave her a hug. There were things I wish I could change in my life, but I knew I had it better than a lot of people, especially Tess.

She laughed and hugged me back. "What's that for?"

I kissed her on the cheek. "I'm just glad you're so wonderfully normal."

"Thanks. I think."

I leaned on the counter. "Darby's helping me with a cheerleading project."

"Really? You're sure it's not too much for her? She's taking those classes. . . ." Mom's face took on that look it always does when Darby's name comes up. Kind of anxious and faraway.

"I don't think so. She acted like she wanted to." I picked up another towel to help her dry the dishes.

I watched my mom closely as she plunged her hands back into the sink and started to scrub at a glass dish. "We just don't want to overtax her. And really, I think we all need to be more careful. We have to stick to the schedule. We can't be lax. You know?"

I nodded but didn't speak. It did no good to try and reassure Mom, because we all knew that no matter how things looked, none of us could really know what was under the surface.

I decided the best course was to change the subject. "Love the hair, by the way."

"Ha. Ha." She touched the pencil she had used to create a messy bun on top of her head. "Occupational hazard." She gave me a small smile, then added, "I was in your room today."

"Yeah."

"What happened to all the pictures?"

"Todd and I broke up. For good. Finis."

"Want to elaborate?"

"Nothing interesting to tell. Is Dad home yet?"

"No. That's it?"

"I never got to see him. It just got to be kind of pointless, you know?"

"You and your invisible guy. Well, maybe now you'll date someone your dad and I can actually meet."

"Yeah, maybe. I'm going to finish my homework." I went upstairs to my room, which still looked odd without the pictures. Mom and Dad had long called Todd the "invisible guy" because somehow, every time they were about to meet him, something would happen and he wouldn't be able to come. Funny how that always happened.

At school, I'd told people that Todd lived next door to my grandparents and that we were super serious. My family thought Todd was a kid from school who had moved away soon after we got together, and that it wasn't very serious. I usually got a headache just thinking about it all. But now I was free. Totally free.

I dropped onto my bed and stared at the ceiling, thoughts of Liam interspersed with thoughts of what Tess was facing at home. Tess had sworn me to secrecy years ago, and I had never really considered breaking the promise until recently. Not only because things were obviously getting worse, but because Tess was growing more and more determined to handle it all on her own. Being a mother to Ashley, taking care of their house, making sure that no one found out that her mom was always either drunk or passed out, and still trying to be a great cheerleader, friend, and—until she dumped Alex—girlfriend.

Tess was amazing, but she was showing signs of stress. For one, she was losing weight. Tess had always been slender and strong—cheerleading did that to a girl—but lately her face seemed thinner, and her uniform was just a bit too big. Not enough for anyone but me to notice probably.

But what scared me was the custody thing with Ashley. Tess had never talked about that. She was making long-range plans as if her mother was never going to improve. As if she had decided that this is what life was going to be, and she was going to have to make the best of it.

On top of that was the fact that her best friend was a huge liar—it made it all that much more depressing. Of course, things were going to be different for me now.

I just wished that things could be different for her, too.

CHAPTER 5

It was B Day and Friday, and I was completely conflicted. I wanted to avoid Liam, embarrassed by whatever information he had heard about me. But I didn't want to just walk away either. Did I have the nerve to ask him out? A simple, casual date? Supposedly people did that sort of thing all the time. And I couldn't shake Tess's admonition that if Liam decided to date someone like Lexi, they may never break up. Plus, I was thinking about him nonstop. What was so special about him, anyway? He was just another guy, but totally *not* at the same time.

It made no sense.

If I asked him out, at least I'd know one way or the other. That would be better than nothing. Hopefully.

Tess picked me up, and I confessed my plan. I knew if I told her, she'd pester me until I did it.

Tess was all for it.

"What can I do?" she asked.

"Nothing. Just make sure I do it."

I wanted to tell her how scared I was, but that would also mean admitting how inexperienced I really was. She didn't need any more drama in her life. Nope, I'd just have to be confident . . . somehow.

Tess had the fund-raiser on her mind. Darby had left messages but was still trying to talk to the right people about getting the space. We couldn't set an exact date until we got the location nailed down, so we were waiting on Darby for several things. Olivia had agreed to handle the money for us. Katie and even Yvie and Sophie had all agreed to help.

"I was thinking we should dress up as elves," Tess said on the way into school.

"Elves? You mean like pointy hat and shoes elves? C'mon, Tess."

"It would look really cute. Besides, the Santa guy we're using said he has some extra elf costumes if we're interested. Gratis."

"We'd look ridiculous."

"It won't matter, because you'll already be dating Liam. After a few dates, you can afford to look ridiculous for one afternoon. Maybe we can get him into a costume, too."

"Tess! I haven't even asked him out yet."

She waved me off. "Minor detail." She leaned in close and whispered, "He'd be crazy to say no."

A rush of warmth went through me. Tess always knew exactly what I needed.

After homeroom we hurried off to get to trig early. But when I got there, I saw Lexi leaning on the wall just outside the classroom. She caught my eye and shifted her body away from me, but I went up to her, anyway.

"Hey, Lexi. I'm glad you're here. I . . . wanted to apologize. For PE the other day."

Lexi looked surprised. "Thanks." She also looked uncomfortable and kept scanning the hallway. "I'm sorry, too."

She had to be waiting for Liam. So did I wait out here to catch him first or just go in and wait in there?

I spotted him about the same time Lexi did. Her face perked up, and she turned toward him. I shifted a little, too, so that we stood there side by side. Liam approached slowly, looking back and forth between us and obviously becoming more uncomfortable with each step he took.

I would not stoop to looking desperate. And I couldn't afford to be worried about what Liam may or may not have heard about me. I didn't know much about guys; but I knew that if I didn't talk to him, show him that I was interested, he'd probably pick someone else. A girl like Lexi. Who was standing there wearing an expression that I wanted to avoid at all costs. Could she be any more obvious?

"Hey, Liam," I chirped. I tried not to, but that's how it came out.

"I wanted to talk to you," Liam said to me.

Lexi's mouth dropped open but only for a second.

"Hi, Lexi," Liam said to her before turning back to me.

The warning bell rang, and the commotion in the hallway amped up a notch as everyone scrambled to get to their classes.

Lexi mumbled something about her class and ducked away.

Score one for me.

Liam stepped closer, and I was taken aback by how good he smelled. Shampoo? Cologne? I had no idea, but I had a hard time not closing my eyes and just breathing him in. Although keeping my eyes open wasn't bad at all. Tanned skin, strong jaw, hair that fell into his face just enough to be cute without being sloppy. He was close enough for me to see a small scar above his left eyebrow.

He fumbled with his earbuds and tucked them into his pocket. "I'm really sorry. I feel horrible about the other night. I should know better than to believe a bunch of rumors."

The hallway emptied, and we stepped inside the classroom.

"That's okay."

"It's not okay. I'd like to make it up to you. . . ."

"Take your seats!" Mr. Petrini called out, and started passing around our quizzes.

Liam gave me a smile. "Can we talk after?"

I nodded, and we sat down. I knew Tess would be expecting an update, but I couldn't tear my eyes from Liam.

He took his paper, then leaned over to get something out of his backpack. As he searched his bag, he frowned with this adorable look of concentration. I think I actually swooned a little. His bag was stuffed full of what looked like sheet music, and a pair of drumsticks poked out of a front pocket. Hanging from the zipper was a backstage pass of some sort. I couldn't see a band name. He shoved his iPod into another pocket, and I wondered what kind of music was on it.

He wants to talk. That's good. But I was still nowhere close to asking him out. Talking to him was taking every bit of courage I had.

Trig was usually excruciating, but even after the quiz was turned in, Mr. Petrini seemed to take particular joy in dragging out the ninety-minute block to its extreme.

When the bell rang, I jumped from my chair and walked toward Liam without a plan in my head.

He turned and gave me a smile. "You have lunch next, right?"

"Yep." *Could I be any less articulate?*

"Mind if I sit with you?"

"Sure."

We walked toward the cafeteria together, but I couldn't get my brain working. *Say something already.*

I spotted Tess talking to Yvie and a couple of other girls, and she gave me a silent cheer.

"So what do we do?" Liam asked.

"About what?"

"Well, you usually sit with Tess, and I usually sit with Alex. But I doubt Tess will want to sit anywhere near Alex if even half of what he told me is true."

"Good point."

Liam turned and looked at me with those soft brown eyes. "We could sit by ourselves. Would Tess mind?"

Would Tess *mind*? She'd probably give me a medal. "I don't think so."

Liam walked up to one of the smaller tables by the window and dropped his notebook on one of the seats. "Is this all right?"

"Sure." I dropped my bag onto another chair and walked with him to get food. I stuck to the salad line, and he got in the grease line. *So what if he eats garbage?*

Tess was with some other cheerleaders, and she gave me a wave, letting me know that she would sit somewhere else.

I got back to the seats first, but Liam didn't take long. He sat down with his tray of fried chicken, mashed potatoes, and, thankfully, a side salad.

"So, you're one of those healthy eaters?" he asked.

"Cheerleading. It's a lot more work if you don't eat right."

Liam looked at his tray and frowned. "It just tastes so

good." He picked up one of the legs. "Come on, try it." He held it out in front of me.

"No way."

Liam laughed. "It won't kill you. One bite. Come on."

"I hardly know you, and you're trying to clog my arteries?"

"Come on," he urged.

"Hey, Liam."

I didn't even have to turn around to know that Lexi was standing right behind me.

"Hi, Lexi." Liam set the chicken leg back down on his tray.

"Mind if I sit with you guys?" she asked.

"Uhhh, sure," he said. What else was he supposed to say? But my heart felt as if it had dropped to the floor.

I managed to keep from letting out the groan I felt inside.

I looked around for Tess and caught her attention. She scowled when she saw Lexi settling herself in the chair next to Liam. I was trying to decide who had the advantage—me across from Liam, or Lexi next to him—when Tess appeared at the end of our table.

"Sorry to interrupt you two, but I need to borrow Lexi."

"Excuse me?" Lexi asked.

"Tammy over at Hope House says that you volunteer there sometimes." Tess was all sweetness and smiles. She was my hero.

"I did over the summer."

"Perfect!" Tess clapped her hands together. "We're putting together a toy drive for Hope House, and I thought you might like to help us."

The girl was brilliant. Lexi glanced at Tess, then Liam,

and then me. She wouldn't be able to refuse without looking bad.

"Sure." She stood up very slowly. "I guess I'll see you later."

Tess put her arm around Lexi and steered her away. Now *that's* a best friend.

"A toy drive?" Liam asked.

I told him about Tess's plan. "Let me know if you need some more help," he offered.

"I'm sure Tess would love any extra help we can get."

Now was my chance. I had to do something, especially after two close calls with Lexi. She was positioning herself well, and she would see Liam at church—a place where she would have the definite advantage. How was I supposed to do this? Blurt it out?

"I think Lexi has a crush on you." *Total fail!*

Liam looked over to where Tess and Lexi were sitting.

"Really?" he asked.

I couldn't tell if he was flattered or simply surprised. He turned back to me. "What about you?"

"What about me what?" *Can he tell I have a crush on him?* I swear I stopped breathing for a second.

"Now that we've established you don't have a boy-friend. . . ."

"I wouldn't be sitting here with you if I did, now would I?" Not a bad response. At least it didn't give away how flustered I was. Did that mean he might be interested?

"True."

Awkward silence.

At least it was awkward for me. I picked at my salad, trying to figure out the right phrasing to make asking him out sound like something I had just randomly thought of. But with the churning in my stomach, I was afraid I might throw up in the process. *Pretend boyfriends are so much easier.*

"So, do you have any plans this weekend?" Liam asked me.

My heart jumped. "I'm cheering tonight. Home game."

"What about after the game? Do you want to catch a late movie or something?"

"Sure, that sounds great." I hoped that the silly grin I felt inside wasn't actually on my face. I had a feeling it probably was.

The bell rang.

I felt like doing a cheer but refrained. Score two for me. And I didn't even have to do the asking.

I stood at Tess's Jeep and waited for her to cross the parking lot.

"You are my hero. My knight in shining armor. My . . ."

"Yeah, yeah, yeah. But did you do the deed?"

"No."

"What? Mallory!"

"He asked me out."

Tess squealed and grabbed my shoulders. "Details."

I told her everything, complete with reenactments.

Tess squealed again. "I can't believe you have a date with a real, live guy! And he's hot! Good grief, it's about time."

I pulled away and stared at her. "What do you mean?"

Tess leaned on her door. "Mallory."

"Mallory what?" I couldn't read her expression.

Tess folded her arms. "Mallory. That whole thing with Todd? I mean, come on, I'm not an idiot."

I stared at her, trying to get my head around what she was saying.

"Tess . . ."

"It's over now. Over and done and gone, and you're moving on, and that's all that matters." Tess climbed into the Jeep and put down the window. "Aren't you coming?"

I was still stunned. "You knew?"

"Look, Mallory. I know all about needing something to be true that isn't. I'm the Queen of Appearances. You know that. I knew you'd get rid of Todd when you were ready."

I couldn't move. Couldn't think. Tess knew that Todd was a figment of my imagination? That he was some made-up boyfriend? I flicked through all the times we had gone shopping because I was going to see Todd and all the phone calls I'd pretended to get and all the weekend wedding trips I went on with my dad just to say I had gone to see him.

I am the most horrible person alive.

I didn't know what else to do but walk away. I wanted to crawl in a hole and never come out again.

"Mallory, wait. Mallory!"

Tess caught up with me, but I kept walking, letting the tears stream down my face.

"Stop, please."

I obeyed and wiped at my face. A girl crying in a high school parking lot wasn't exactly noteworthy, but I was still self-conscious—a lot of people were hanging around.

"I didn't mean to make you cry. I figured it was okay now. . . . You took down the pictures."

I tried to wrestle control of my emotions. Tess *knew.*

Tess knew and wasn't angry or even hurt. So why was I the one bawling like a baby?

I was embarrassed. Actually, embarrassed didn't go far enough—*humiliated* would be a better word. It was like being blissfully unaware of the fact that you'd been parading around with your skirt tucked into your underwear.

Tess looked worried and a little confused.

"Why?" I choked out the question. "Why did you let me lie to you?"

Tess gave me a small smile. "Because you weren't hurting anyone. I have to lie all the time for my mom, and she hurts us every day. You? I don't know. I guess I just wanted you to be happy."

Tess hugged me and pulled me back to the Jeep. "Now get in. Remember the rule? No more talking about Todd. It's over."

I sat there, wrung out and slightly relieved. Tess knew the truth and still loved me. What more could a girl ask for?

CHAPTER 6

I could ask for a lot, apparently. The top thing being that Lexi would transfer to another school district. She not only came to the game but planted herself and a couple of her friends on the bleachers right in front of the squad. I swear, every time I had to shake my hips I got a look of judgment from her.

Tess noticed, too. During a water break she asked, "Does she usually come to the games?"

I shook my head. "Not that I know of." I had yet to see Liam, but it was still the first quarter.

"Lexi's harmless. Liam asked you out, not her. She'll get over it." Tess trotted back to her spot.

I hoped she was right.

Just then I caught sight of Liam strolling through the crowds toward the bleachers. He caught my eye and made his way to the fence line where I was standing.

"Hey, you. Still up for tonight?" He leaned on the metal fence, a killer smile across his face.

"Yeah. I like your jacket." I reached out to touch the soft brown leather, and he rested his hand on top of mine. Shivers went through me as well as a shot of fear. I didn't know what to do on a date. *What will I say? How will I act?*

"Mallory!" someone from the squad shouted.

I heard the music start. "Gotta go!" I ran off, looking back as I jumped into my spot. He was still leaning in the same position, watching.

I knew the routine cold, so as I spun and cartwheeled and jumped around, I was able to keep track of Liam. First he was just standing there watching me. Then I saw Lexi walking down the bleachers. *Then* she was standing next to him. And by the time the dance was over, she had moved him up into the bleachers right beside her.

How dare she? She'd snaked him away all in the span of a four-minute song.

I stood next to Tess, who had her arms crossed and was scowling in Lexi's general direction.

"She's got nerve, doesn't she?" Tess said.

"Yeah, and she's using it on Liam. Aren't there a hundred other guys in this school?"

"She's probably thinking the same thing about you."

"Not helpful."

"Why are you even worried about it? Remember, he asked *you* out."

The music started again, and I moved into my place, never taking my eyes off Liam and Lexi. She seemed to be talking to him while he watched the game. And me. He was definitely looking in my direction, and he smiled several times, too. It should have been enough to reassure me, but it wasn't.

And the game going into overtime didn't help. Liam looked at his cell phone several times, and I knew a movie was going to be out of the question if the game didn't end in the next ten minutes.

I turned toward the field, willing someone—anyone—on

our team to score and end the agony. Tess walked over and stood next to me.

"You don't have to see a movie. It'd be better to go somewhere you can talk, anyway."

I nodded.

The opposing team fumbled, and the crowd reacted with a gasp. One of our players snatched the ball and began running, and we all started yelling as we watched him dodge the other players and cross into the end zone.

We turned and shook our pom-poms in the air at the crowd. Liam and Lexi were both on their feet but were looking at each other, engrossed in a conversation.

A moment later Lexi turned and started moving, working her way down the bleachers with Liam following her.

Tess and I went to gather our bags, everyone in high spirits because of the win. Me, I felt sick to my stomach. How can you want something so badly and be totally scared of it at the exact same time?

Tess put her arm around me and squeezed my shoulders. "Have fun and call me the second it's over. Promise?"

"Promise."

She walked away with a couple of other girls from the squad. I checked my cell phone and immediately wished I hadn't. Three texts, all from Mom, expecting me to be back home by nine to stay with Darby. It was already after eight.

I stared at the texts. *It will be fine. Darby will be fine.* Right?

For the first time in my life, I had an adorable guy with a smile on his face waiting for me.

I'll only be a little late. I shoved my phone into my bag and walked toward Liam.

"Hey, you," I said.

He smiled. Even with all my fluttery nerves, I was so happy that smile was for me.

"I think we missed the movie," he said. "Are you hungry? We could get something to eat."

"Sure." I fell in step next to him.

"Where do you want to go?"

I considered that. The typical after-football hangouts would be crowded and uncomfortable for a first date. But the non-hangout places would be too quiet. Decisions were not my forte.

We'd made it all the way to Liam's car, and I still couldn't figure out the best place to go.

"Maybe Roxy's?"

"That's the one on Courthouse?" he asked.

"Yeah." Roxy's would be crowded but probably not as bad as some other places.

It took a while to get out of the parking lot, so it wasn't until we got onto the road that he turned and looked at me.

"That was some impressive stuff you did out there."

"Oh, I can only do the basics. Tara's the one who does the really fancy moves."

"I guess I didn't realize how many stunts cheerleaders do."

"Don't go to many games, huh?"

"Football seems bigger here than at the last place I lived. I figured I'd try to have the whole experience since I'll be able to stay and graduate here."

"You will?"

"Yeah."

"Where'd you live before this?"

"Connecticut. Hockey was the game to play up there. I

even learned to ice-skate, but I never got good enough to actually make a team. Before that it was South Carolina."

"Do you play any sports?"

"Not really. I guess I'm more into music." He said it apologetically.

"Like what kind?"

"All kinds. I play the piano and guitar, and I'm learning to play the drums."

"Wow. That's pretty impressive, too."

He smiled at the compliment, then pulled the car into the parking lot of Roxy's. It was way more crowded than I thought it would be.

We went inside and ordered some drinks.

It wasn't going badly. Liam was easy to talk to, and since we didn't know each other, asking questions was just natural. *So far, so good.*

I wanted to bring up Lexi, just to see what his reaction would be, but it seemed like a desperate thing to do. No reason to let on that I was concerned about her.

"What about you? You grew up here?" he asked.

"Pretty much."

"And your family?"

"Older sister. Mom and dad. All pretty normal." At least that's the way it looked to everyone else. It was kind of strange to realize that I couldn't be totally honest with him, even though I swore I wouldn't lie anymore. Keeping my family secrets from Todd was easy, of course, but what about a real boyfriend?

Enough! It was just our first date, and I was already stressing over what secrets I was allowed to keep from a boyfriend.

"Normal's okay. Actually, normal can be great." Liam

looked at me, I mean, *really* looked at me, like he was trying to see something inside of me. His eyes were the color of milk chocolate, and I wanted to reach over and brush his hair out of the way.

Then I happened to glance up and see Lexi coming through the door with a couple of other girls. I rolled my eyes, and Liam turned to look over his shoulder.

"I think she's stalking you," I said. And ticking me off.

"Don't worry about it," he said.

I didn't *want* to worry about it, but she was making a beeline for our table. I sat back in the bench seat as she stopped at the end of the table.

"Funny running into you two here," she said.

"Hilarious," I said.

Liam looked at her. "I think your friends are waiting for you." He pointed to the booth they had grabbed near the windows.

"Oh, they can wait. I was going to ask if I could get a ride to church on Sunday." Lexi smiled at him, a picture of feigned innocence.

Liam cleared his throat and looked at me. I tried to act uninterested, but my whole body tensed, waiting to see what he would do. *I will not kill Lexi.*

"Sure. I guess so."

"Thanks!" Lexi grabbed his hand. "That'll be such a help." She bounced off, and he turned his attention back to me.

"Sorry about that."

I wasn't sure what he was sorry about. Lexi? Giving her a ride?

"We're just friends, in case you're wondering," he added.

"I think she'd like to be more than friends."

Liam fixed his eyes on me. "I'm more interested to know how you feel."

I felt my cheeks grow hot as he took my hand in his. "About . . . ?"

He grinned. "This. You. Me."

"I'm pretty interested."

He picked up my hand and kissed it. "Glad to hear it. Because I am, too."

Now I was positive that there was a silly grin on my face, but I didn't care.

The crowded restaurant seemed to disappear as we talked. I found out all sorts of things about him. He was the younger of two and was probably grossly underplaying his musical talent. I found myself wanting to hear him sing.

And he seemed genuinely interested in me. I told him about my family—leaving out the bits about Darby, of course—and about my friendship with Tess. By the time we left, I was no closer to understanding why I liked him so much, but I was surer than ever that I wanted to be around him. As much as possible.

Then we got in the car and I saw the time. *Ten o'clock?* Panic set in immediately. I couldn't bring myself to even look at my phone.

I gave Liam a smile. "I need to get home. Quick."

CHAPTER 7

He drove fast and mercifully didn't ask any questions. As he pulled into the driveway, I saw my dad running up the porch stairs with a flashlight. He stopped when he saw the car.

"Thanks, Liam. I had a really good time, but I'd better go," I said.

"Can I do anything to help?"

"No. No. Everything's fine. I'll see you tomorrow." I jumped out of the car and hurried over to Dad. He pressed his hand to his mouth, his eyes wide.

Mom pushed open the front door. "Thank God . . . wait. Darby's not with you?"

I shook my head.

Mom grabbed the flashlight from my dad's hands. "Where the hell have you been?" She took off down the front steps and started up the sidewalk.

I looked at Dad. "I'm sorry. . . . I didn't mean to be this late."

"I just got here myself. We've searched the house, and her car's still here. Any ideas?"

I couldn't handle the fear in my dad's eyes, so I looked at the ground and really thought. It was dark, so she wouldn't walk in the woods. But why would she walk *anywhere* at this hour? Maybe she wasn't getting better like I thought.

But this time I was the fool. Mom had been trying to warn me, and I didn't listen.

I bit back the tears. Dad rubbed my shoulder. "It's okay. I'm sure she's fine. I'm going to go find your mom." Dad went down the stairs.

"What can I do?" I asked.

"Find her." He disappeared into the darkness, and I went inside. I threw my bag near the stairs and turned my cell phone back on. Maybe Darby had called or texted.

But all I found, other than texts from Tess, were seven texts and two very upset voice mails from my mom. I deleted them. All of them.

I went to the back porch and looked toward the woods. *Is she out there?* But then I remembered something. When Darby first got home from the hospital, she'd go to the elementary school a lot. To the left of the building was a creek and an outcropping of rocks that she'd sit on for hours. I couldn't remember the last time she'd gone there, but it was worth a shot. I grabbed a flashlight and ran outside, where my mom and dad were having a quiet but fierce conversation.

Mom was crying. I tried to tell myself that she was just worried, but it didn't help.

"I have an idea where to look," I said, running past them.

I heard my dad protesting behind me, but I kept going. My cell phone buzzed, and I answered it, thinking it could be Darby.

But it was Tess.

"What happened?! I've been dying!" she said.

Liam seemed a million miles away at that moment. "Great."

"Great? That's it?"

"More than great."

"Okay, now we're getting somewhere. Are you running on a treadmill or something?"

I slowed my pace as I turned the corner and approached the school. Under the glow of the parking lot lights, I could see Darby walking toward me. I swallowed a relieved sob that came out of nowhere.

"Lexi was there," I choked out, trying to pull my emotions back in before Darby got to me.

"We have to put a monitoring device on Lexi. She could be a significant problem. And speaking of significant problems, can I come over again tonight?"

Darby came up to me, looking confused but perfectly normal. Perfectly safe. I smiled at Darby and turned my attention back to Tess. "Can you give me twenty minutes?" I asked.

"See you then!" Tess said.

I hung up the call and texted my dad:

Found her!

"You saw my note?" Darby asked.

"Yeah," I lied. "It was just getting so late."

We started back home. "I didn't realize that much time had passed, and I forgot my cell. Sorry about that."

"No big deal," I said. Another lie.

"How was the game? I need to come watch you cheer sometime."

"It was good. I know you're so busy with school."

Darby laughed lightly. "Just two classes."

"But it's something."

We got home and found Dad at the counter with his

laptop and my mom sitting at the table grading papers. As if they didn't have a care in the world.

"Hey, Darby!" Mom said.

I walked into the kitchen and casually scanned the countertops while my mom asked Darby about school. I didn't find it until I got to the fridge—a note stuck next to the ice dispenser: *Hey guys, Taking a walk to the school. Be back soon. Love, Darby*

I pulled the note from the fridge, and when Darby turned away for a moment, I tossed it in front of my mom and left the room.

I found Tess sitting on the front porch, waiting. "Sorry," she said. "Had to get out of there." She turned, revealing a red, swollen cheek.

"Tess, what *happened*?"

I dragged her inside and sent her up to my room. Swinging by the kitchen, where Darby was still talking to Mom, I dug around in the freezer for a bag of frozen peas. Dad raised his eyebrow at me, but I just smiled at him and ran up to my room.

Tess was sitting at my computer desk looking at a project I'd been working on. "What's this?" she asked.

"A new logo for the wrestling team. Do you like it?"

"Yeah, it's great. How do you come up with this stuff?"

"I don't know." I handed her the peas, and she gave me a funny look. "Just put it on your cheek. My mom always used these as ice packs." I sat down on my bed. "What happened?"

Tess shook her head. "It was my own fault."

"I don't believe that for a minute, Tess."

"It was. Darren was over again, and he was being drunk and stupid, and he kind of hit on me."

"Kind of hit on you?" Darren was her mother's on-again, off-again, sleazy boyfriend.

"I shoved him when he got too close, and my mom backhanded me. I should have just left."

I looked at her closely, trying to measure how much of the story I was getting. "Tess, this has got to stop. What about Ashley?"

"Ashley's at a friend's house. She's fine." Tess adjusted the peas and leaned back on the chair. "Sorry to ruin your first-date high."

"Tess. Nothing's more important than you."

"They'll sleep it off. She probably won't even remember it in the morning."

"You will." I sat down on the bed and turned to face her. "We've got to do something. What if he tries something on Ashley? She's not as strong as you are."

"He wouldn't dare. I'd kill him." Tess's eyes were hard. I knew it wasn't just a figure of speech.

"There's got to be somewhere you can go for help."

"I told you. There's nothing I can do. If I report it they'll put us both in foster care, probably apart. Do you have any idea what the foster care system is like?" Tess's words were quick and angry.

"We have to do something," I said, more to myself but still out loud.

"I've looked at every alternative. I just have to get through eighteen months. That's it. That's the plan. That, and staying out of Darren's way." Tess moved the peas from her face. "How bad does it look?"

I cringed. "It's gonna bruise. What will you say?"

"That I tripped and fell. Easy breezy."

On Saturday Tess refused to talk anymore about getting help, so to take her mind off everything, I suggested shopping. When we came downstairs, Darby was chopping up fruit for a smoothie. "Wow. What happened? Get kicked by one of those cheerleaders?" she asked.

"If only." Tess climbed onto a stool. "Any word on a spot?"

Darby blended the drink, then poured the pink mixture into a glass. "Actually, yes. I got a callback from one leasing agency, and it looks promising. But they need to get an okay from corporate to officially let us use it. Of course, if they manage to rent it before, then they'll cancel on us, but it's sat empty for nearly a year."

"What's the address? I'd like to swing by and take a look."

Darby handed Tess a piece of paper. "I'm still talking to two others, just in case. I figured we'd better have a backup plan."

"You're awesome, Darby!" Tess turned to me. "Do you mind if we do a drive-by before we hit the mall?"

"Sure." I glanced at Darby, trying to gauge whether we should invite her. I kind of wanted to be alone with Tess, knowing she'd never talk in front of Darby. But at the same time, I could hear my mom's instructions echoing in my head. "What are you doing today?" I asked her.

Darby shrugged. "I'll probably finish working on my essay. I'm good," she said.

"Is Mom home?" I asked.

"She's on the elliptical downstairs. Why?"

"Oh, no reason," I said. *Just need to escape before she comes up, that's all.*

"Well, go and have fun then," Darby urged. She smiled at me, and I caught a faint glimpse of the old Darby. It was happening more often, I was sure, but I couldn't just forget the danger either. Especially after last night.

No one outside the family was supposed to know about Darby. Some people knew a few things: that she was sick, that my parents were worried, that she had dropped out of school. All of it true, but it was only part of the story.

Darby had gone away to the University of Virginia to study art history. She had always wanted to become a curator or professor. I was busy with high school, so for a while I hadn't even realized there were problems, but both Mom and Dad grew more and more anxious when Darby would call home. Then during Christmas break last year everything went haywire.

Darby had come home sick. Not just with a cold or even the flu, but really, really sick. She had failed her first semester, and it turned out that she had been sick off and on the whole time, missing classes but refusing to see a doctor. My parents had thought it was appendicitis because she was doubled over in pain. They had to force her into the car to get her to the emergency room. It turned out to be a pelvic infection. She had gotten an STD, and since she had never been treated, the infection spread into her pelvis. She ended up in emergency surgery and was told soon after that she may never be able to have children.

The news devastated her. And my parents. Even as she had been healing from the surgery, she was distraught, crying all the time.

In February she'd overdosed on her pain pills.

I was the one who had found her after school that day, limp and unresponsive, her long brown hair spilling in every direction on the linoleum floor of the bathroom. I could still picture the scene in my head, like I saw it in a movie instead of in real life. I had never been more scared. Screaming her name, shaking her, calling the paramedics. It was all a blur. I'd ridden in the ambulance with her since Mom and Dad weren't home, and I'd watched the paramedics fight to get her stabilized, yelling things I didn't understand. I sat there numb, trying to imagine what would happen if she didn't wake up. Realizing that she might die.

But she didn't die, and after a seven-day stay in a psych hospital, she came home on antidepressants and with strict instructions for us to keep an eye on her. It was the spring and summer of no light. I'd basically been assigned to be Darby's babysitter, even though, being three years older, she had always been the one looking after me.

Sometimes I was so angry about it I could hardly think, especially when Darby would lie in front of the TV for days on end. But other times, like when I'd find her curled up in a closet sobbing, I'd desperately wanted to help her, fix her, anything.

Fake Todd had come along during the worst part of it all. Todd was my escape route to say no to parties when I had to stay home with Darby. I'd say I was visiting Todd when we had to go away for Darby's therapy weekends. It was a fantasy world that I desperately needed at a time when I thought things would never get any better. I'd kept everyone at arm's length, except for Tess. Tess was like hot glue. There was no getting rid of Tess even if I had wanted to. She could see that Darby was depressed, but she'd never pried or bugged me for details. And I'd never told her about the suicide attempt. I wasn't trying to keep it from her per se, but the right time to mention it never came.

In the end, it just took time. Darby had decided this fall, on her own, to pick up a few classes at the community college. For the first time, I was starting to see small doses of improvement.

And now she was shooing me out the door. Baby steps, but it was great. I gave her a hug and followed Tess out to her Jeep.

We found the building easily. It looked kind of shabby; but it had plenty of parking and, from what we could see, was big enough inside for what we needed to do.

Tess pointed to the roofline. "Some garland, some lights—we could make this look all festive, couldn't we?"

"Yeah, and that stuff's not too expensive either."

"I hope we can get this one. I like that it's not too far away." Tess wrote down something in the small spiral notebook she'd been carrying around lately. "Is Darby okay with doing all this?"

"I think so." I watched Tess look around with a critical eye. Even with extra makeup I could still see the bruising on her cheek. "I know you're sick of hearing this, Tess, but seriously, I think we need to do something about your mom."

Tess's phone rang, and she lifted an eyebrow at me. "Just had to bring her up, didn't you?"

Tess answered, and I could hear indistinct yelling through the phone. Tess shook her head at me. "I know, Mom. I'm taking care of it. Yes. Yes!" Tess jammed her finger at the phone to hang it up. "We need to make another detour."

We drove toward Tess's house in silence, knowing the shopping trip, no matter how much Tess needed it, probably wouldn't happen. Tess pulled into her driveway and parked the car.

She spoke without looking at me. "You may want to wait in the car. It looks like Darren is still here."

"I want to come with you, but . . . it's up to you." I didn't want to make things any harder on her, but I also didn't want to let her go inside alone.

Tess gave a heavy shrug of her shoulder. "It doesn't matter."

That was enough for me. I followed her up to the door, where she paused before pushing it open.

Darren was sitting in the small living room, a glass beer bottle in his hand, watching TV. He was scrawny and stubbly and dressed in dirty jeans. The shades were all drawn, making the room feel stuffy and dingy.

"Hey, baby." Darren laughed, and wiped his hand across his dirty tank top.

"I'm not your baby," Tess snarled. "Where's Mom?"

"Tessie, is that you?" Her mom's voice carried in from another room.

Tess gave Darren a wide berth and went into the kitchen. I followed the same path and ignored Darren's obvious leering.

Tess's mom was standing in the kitchen, wearing ratty sweatpants and a too-big T-shirt with a fraying robe on top. Her blond hair was hanging in greasy strings, and she had a bruise on her jawline.

"There's no more chips! Darren really wanted to have chips. Why didn't you go to the grocery store?" She was pleading as if she were the kid.

Tess wasn't having any of it. "There's plenty of food, Mom."

"But not the chips Darren likes."

"That's because you need to get Darren out of here, Mom. We talked about this. He can't stay here."

Tess's mom burst into tears. "Why are you doing this to me? Why can't you just be happy for me?" She flung herself from the room, and Tess looked at me. "I've got to take some clothes to Ashley."

I followed Tess to Ashley's bedroom and watched her throw some clothes into a polka-dot bag on the bed.

"Tess."

"Don't, Mallory. I need to do this."

I leaned against the wall. "You are so stubborn."

"I have to be. Once I get Darren out of here again, it'll all calm down. He makes everything ten times worse."

"What will you do?"

Tess lifted her head and smirked. "Call his parole officer. Anonymously, of course. It'll only get rid of him for six months, but I'll take what I can get."

"You're the bravest person I know."

"I don't know about that." Tess zipped up the bag. "That should do it."

Tess drove to Ashley's friend's house and dropped off the bag, then drove toward the mall. On the way, she made the call to the parole officer.

"Will they pick him up?" I asked when she hung up.

"Hopefully."

"You still want to go shopping?" I asked.

"Absolutely. Don't you?"

I shrugged.

"Forget about it, Mallory. You've just got to push it aside and live your life. It's all you can do. Distraction can be a girl's best friend." Tess nudged my shoulder playfully.

My phone rang, and I looked at the display.

"Oh, no. It's Liam," I whispered.

"Answer it."

I stared at the phone until Tess snatched it from my hand and put it to her ear.

"Mallory's phone. Why, yes, she is. No, we're at the mall. Sure, meet us at the food court at one. Okay, bye."

Tess closed the phone.

"What did you do?"

"What? He wanted to get out of the house."

"Tess!"

"What? You said last night was great, that you got along."

"I don't want to make him sick of me." What I didn't say was that I was afraid. Afraid of getting in over my head. Afraid that I couldn't handle a real relationship.

"He called you, you dope. He wants to see you. Embrace it."

I followed Tess into the mall but was slowly working myself into a panic. Last night was as close to perfect as I could imagine. Seeing him again was likely to screw up everything.

The mall was filled with kids from our high school, and the food court was packed. Tess managed to snag a table. She held it while I went to buy our food.

"Hey, Mallory."

I turned to see Jason O'Neill holding a fountain drink as if he was posing for a photo shoot.

"Hi, Jason." I turned my attention to the menu board above me, but Jason sidled up and leaned in close.

"Go out with me."

I laughed. I mean, I couldn't help myself. "Thanks, Jace, but I can't."

"I heard you were available. C'mon. You won't regret it." He slipped a hand onto my hip and tried to pull me closer.

Is he serious? I pulled away. "Excuse me. Personal space." I walked away and heard him call me a nasty name behind my back.

"I think you better go get the food," I said to Tess.

"What did O'Neill want?"

"A hot date, apparently. Which is *not* gonna be me."

"Jason's such a skeeze."

Tess left to get the food, and I tried to gather my thoughts. Jason was already hitting on some other girl in front of Taco Bell, and I felt like I still had his slime on me. I glanced around, hoping to spot Liam, but either he wasn't there yet or I couldn't see him.

Tess came back with a tray and set it between us. "Lexi's here."

"No." I followed Tess's subtle pointing to see Lexi at a table with a couple of other girls. Why was she always showing up and ruining things?

"And Liam, too." Tess nodded behind me, and I turned to see Liam hovering at the edge of the food court, looking around. He saw Lexi first. She was waving at him. But when he didn't move, she jumped from her seat and maneuvered her way through the chairs and tables over to his side.

I groaned.

"Just wait," Tess said. "He'll find you."

Liam and Lexi talked for less than a second before she looped her arm through his and practically dragged him toward her table. I stared at him, trying to send mental messages to turn around and see me. Liam stood at Lexi's table; but despite her pulling out a chair, he didn't sit. He glanced around again and this time caught my eye. He held up one finger in a wait signal.

"See, he's coming," Tess said.

Another eternity later, Liam finally extricated himself from Lexi's table and came to ours and sat down beside me.

"Hey, guys. Sorry about that." He turned to me. "Everything okay?"

I nodded, but Tess was still staring at Lexi. "She just won't leave you alone, will she?" Tess said, with a lot more boldness than I could ever muster.

Liam shrugged and looked . . . maybe embarrassed?

"What's her problem, anyway?" Tess wasn't about to let him off the hook. Go, Tess.

Liam sat back and took a fry from my plate. "She thinks ya'll are a bad influence."

I thought it was so cute the way he said "ya'll" that the actual words didn't register in my head until Tess pounced.

"Excuse me? And since when was she elected the keeper of your conscience?"

"I guess she's worried."

"What did she say?" Tess demanded.

Liam squirmed.

Tess pointed at him. "Spill it."

Liam looked at me for help, but since I wanted to know, too, I wasn't about to bail him out.

"She just said that . . . you're killing me here."

Tess frowned at him.

"Fine." Liam threw his hands up in the air. "She just went on and on about how you have a reputation and that I might be tempted to . . . you know . . . if I continue to see you. She thinks that I need a girl . . ."

"Like her?" I asked.

"Who's going to respect my beliefs," he finished.

Tess and I sat there for a long second. Even without saying it out loud, I knew what he was talking about. Tess jumped up and, in determined strides, headed right for Lexi's table.

"Oh, no." I pushed my chair back and followed her.

Tess planted her hands on Lexi's table. "I need to talk to you. *Alone.*"

Lexi definitely had some fear playing around her eyes. Tess could be very menacing when she needed to be. Lexi stood up, eye to eye with Tess. "Anything you have to say to me, you can say in front of them. They're my friends."

"I'm surprised you have any, what with being such a gossiper. Tell me. Do you go around spreading lies about them, too, or just Mallory?"

"I don't spread lies."

"Oh, really? You seem to be campaigning awfully hard to get Liam all to yourself."

"I'm just trying to protect him."

"From Mallory?" Tess laughed.

I watched in horror as, one by one, people at the tables surrounding us turned to stare and listen.

"Yes. It's no secret that Mallory's one of *those* girls."

"*Those* girls?"

"Yeah." Lexi swallowed hard but squared her shoulders. "Girls who think sex is just some extracurricular activity. Well, I don't think that, and neither does Liam. He has a right to know."

I felt my cheeks grow hot and my stomach go sour.

Tess's eyes were wild and angry. "So you think being a virgin makes you a better person? Better than Mallory?

Better than me? I'll tell you something, Lexi Taylor. Seems to me that being a virgin has made you into a self-righteous little brat. You're not some saint because you don't have sex. And I'm not some kind of pariah because I have. You didn't waste a second before trying to tear Mallory down to get what you want. I think you should be less worried about sex and more worried about being a better human being. Even God would appreciate that." Tess leaned in close. "Leave Mallory alone."

Tess took my elbow and steered me back to our table. I could hear murmurs behind us, but I didn't want to turn and look. We sat down, and I buried my face in my arms.

"I'm sorry, Mallory, I had to do it. That little . . . she can't lie about you and get away with it."

"I'm not mad at you. I'm mad at me. I've made a mess of everything." I looked over to where Liam had been standing during the confrontation, but there was no sign of him now. "Great. He's gone."

"He'll be back." Tess patted my arm. "He just needs time to think."

"But, Tess, she didn't lie."

"Yes, she did. She doesn't know anything about you. She doesn't know what kind of person you are. Liam would be lucky to have you. And since Todd was . . . you know . . . I'm assuming that you couldn't have had sex with him. You're not one of *those* girls, Mallory. And you shouldn't be ashamed of it."

"But I am. I've been lying to everyone about everything, all to get a reputation that's going to spoil my chances with the one guy I really like."

"So tell him the truth."

"I can't."

"Why not?"

I considered that for like a nanosecond, but admitting to my fictional relationship wasn't even an option. "He'll think I'm crazy."

"You don't have to tell him about Todd. Just about being a virgin."

"But that shouldn't matter, should it?"

"Maybe to him it does."

I shook my head. "I don't know. . . ."

Tess smiled sympathetically. "I still think he'll be back."

I hoped she was right. *But how will I ever face him?*

CHAPTER 8

And then there was my mother, who was waiting for me when Tess and I got back to my house. She didn't say a word, but I knew I was going to have to talk to her.

Up in my room, I got Tess to look at some websites so she could show me what she had in mind for the fund-raiser posters. I told her I'd be back and then went to the kitchen.

Better just to get it over with.

Mom pointed at a chair with her pencil, and I sat down.

"You were supposed to be back by nine. None of that would have happened if you had been here."

"She left a—"

"I don't care that she left a note. You were supposed to be here." Mom's voice was low but angry.

I pulled back my own anger and didn't say the twenty things that flooded my thoughts. That we shouldn't have to live like this. That Darby was fine. That Mom was probably overreacting.

"You're grounded," she said.

"Grounded? Are you serious?" I stood up, pushing the chair back hard.

Mom's eyes flashed. "If I say you need to be here, then you need to be here. There is no discussion. I think your sister's life is worth it, don't you?"

I could feel my hands trembling, as if I was ready to

explode, so I did the only thing I could. I left the room. I had nowhere to go to gather my thoughts or emotions so I locked myself in the bathroom, the room that haunted me on a regular basis, and curled up in the corner. I didn't cry. I couldn't afford the red eyes when I got back into the room with Tess. Tess had enough going on in her life already.

I took long, slow breaths, trying to calm down. Trying to ignore the hole where one of the paramedics had slammed something into the wall when he was trying to save Darby's life. Once my breathing was normal and I didn't feel as if I was on the edge of tears, I went back to my room.

"We should go out tonight!" Tess said.

"I don't feel like it." I didn't tell her that I was grounded.

"You cannot stay cooped up inside. Besides, a little birdy told me that there's some concert at Liam's church. I bet he'll be there."

"Yeah. With Lexi. Haven't we had enough drama for one day?"

"Nah. It's high school. It's all about the drama." She grinned, then folded her hands and begged.

"Since when do you want to go to church?"

Tess shrugged. "They can't all be like Lexi."

"Well, I'm not going to stalk him. He has my phone number, right?"

Tess gave a heavy sigh. "Fine, fine, fine. Then we're going to do fund-raiser planning. I'll make you work all night."

She probably thought it would convince me to go out. Instead, it was the perfect plan.

"Deal," I said.

The next morning I woke up early. Since Tess was still sleeping, I crept out of the room, went onto the back porch with a blanket, and curled up in the lounge chair. It was chilly, and the leaves were just beginning to turn to yellows and oranges for fall. The woods running behind our house were still and quiet. I didn't spend a lot of time alone, and I found myself enjoying the peacefulness of being out there. Well, until I started thinking about Liam.

It bothered me that he hadn't called, but it bothered me a lot more that yesterday had happened at all. Even though I was technically free of Todd, I still didn't feel free. It was as if that lie, and all the baby lies it had made, were following me around. And ruining my chances with Liam.

The door slid open behind me, and I turned to see Darby with a cup of coffee in her hand.

"Oh! I didn't know you were out here. Do you want to be alone?"

I shook my head, and my throat closed up. I could feel the tears pooling in my eyes.

"What's wrong?"

I heard her pull over a chair and sit down as I tried to focus on the woods and get control of my emotions. I wasn't allowed to talk to Darby about anything emotional, but I desperately wanted to. I wanted to tell her everything, to get her advice and help. But I couldn't risk adding any pressure. I was in enough trouble already.

After I knew my eyes were clear, I shifted the conversation. "What are you doing up so early?" I asked.

"This is what I do every morning. I should be asking you that question."

"I couldn't get back to sleep."

"Everything okay?"

"Yeah. So what do you do out here every morning?"

"Drink my coffee. Pray."

Pray. Darby had been going to church, on her own, since early summer. We had never really been a church-going family, though I was pretty sure both of my parents probably believed in God. We had been raised with strong morals, and if I was really honest, choosing not to have sex was probably more about me not disappointing my parents than it was about God. At least at first. Then I just got plain scared after what had happened to Darby. Everything she had been through was because of having sex with the wrong person in college and getting that stupid STD.

I guess I believed in God; I didn't have any reason not to. But I wasn't like Lexi, who talked about God at school and everywhere else she went. I wasn't sure where faith really fit into my life. At least not yet. The Twelve Steps talked a lot about God, about recognizing that you need help from a higher power. I had admitted to Tess that Todd was a fake, which was Step 5, but I felt as though I was still lying about other things. Even sitting here with Darby I wasn't being real.

And I really wanted to be. "What do you pray about?" I asked her.

"Everything."

I watched her as she sipped her coffee, a placid expression on her face. "We get this idea that we can handle most things on our own, then along comes a problem that just seems too big for us," she said.

Tess came to mind.

Darby continued. "God-sized problems. I've had a few of

those. And what I learned was that God's not only interested in the huge ones, he's interested in all of them. So that's what I pray about. Everything."

Darby went back to her coffee; and even though I had a hundred questions, I kept them to myself, letting the quiet settle around us instead.

Once Tess woke up we decided to make pancakes. Ever since we were first able to use the skillet, we'd see how big a pancake we could make without breaking it when we had to flip it. Today was a day for big pancakes.

It was like old times. We were giggling and laughing, and even Dad put in an order for a pancake. Mom came around the corner and gestured for me to follow her into the living room. I handed the spatula over to Tess and went to face my mother.

She had her arms crossed. "You're grounded and Tess slept over?"

"I didn't go anywhere. You didn't say she couldn't stay."

Mom's shoulders relaxed, and she reached out and touched my arm. "Mallory, your dad . . . maybe I *was* too rash in grounding you. I'm just worried."

"About Darby."

"And you. And Tess. She's here an awful lot lately."

"I know."

"So it makes me wonder if things are okay at home. If there's a reason she's here all the time."

I couldn't tell her the truth, but it was obvious she knew something was wrong.

Mom sighed. "Look, I don't mind, but staying here isn't

exactly a long-term solution. We've got Darby to think about. Is there anything I can do?"

I shook my head.

"All right. I'm here if you need me."

I followed her back into the kitchen, where Tess gave me a questioning look. I let her know that it was okay.

Tess got along with us great, and if it were just her, I might have tried to convince my parents to let her move in. But Ashley was another story. I wasn't sure my parents would take custody of a twelve-year-old. Or if they would even be allowed to. Tess was almost old enough to get emancipated, but Ashley wasn't. And it's not as if my parents were certified for foster care or anything. And there was always the Darby situation. But still, I tucked the idea away. It couldn't hurt to ask if things got desperate, as long as I didn't have to divulge any more than necessary.

Darby came into the kitchen ready to leave for church. She was dressed in a nice A-line skirt and blouse and had her hair twisted up into a knot.

"Anyone want to come with me?" she asked.

"I do!" Tess said.

I shot Tess a look.

She shrugged.

"What about you, Mallory?" Darby asked.

Tess grabbed my arm. "We'll be ready in five minutes." She dragged me up the stairs.

"What are you doing, Tessie? Since when do you go to church?"

Tess just smiled and then went to my closet and pulled out clothes for both of us. "Get ready, will ya?"

I gave in. It was easy to slip back into our usual relationship, the one in which Tess made the decisions and I went along for the ride. Maybe my life was distracting her from her own. Whatever it was, the spark in Tess's eyes was stronger than I had seen it in days.

We ran outside to where Darby was waiting in her car, and climbed in.

"I didn't expect you to actually agree to go." Darby glanced in the rearview mirror and caught my eye. "I'm glad you did, though."

Tess didn't say much on the way, and I just sat there trying to figure out if there was something I should do to prepare to go to church. I knew Darby's church was different from the one my parents had taken us to occasionally, so I wasn't quite sure what to expect. I thought about asking, but suddenly we were there and climbing out of the car. And I saw Lexi standing in a small group by one of the doors.

I got back into the car and slammed the door shut.

Both Darby and Tess stopped. They had a short conversation, and Tess climbed back in the car.

"You are evil and rotten," I said.

"I didn't know!" She put one hand on her chest and held up two fingers with the other. "Girl Scout promise."

"Oh, and I'm supposed to believe that you just suddenly wanted to go to church with my sister for no reason. That you had no idea that this is Liam's church!"

Tess raised an eyebrow. "Now, now. Are you really the one to scold me about telling stories?"

I scowled at her. "I've had enough humiliation, thank you very much."

"You have nothing to be humiliated about. It's a church. As far as I know, everyone's welcome. Including you."

I closed my eyes, wishing desperately I had never come. "You had to have known," I said.

"All right, I knew where Liam went to church, but I didn't know that this is the one Darby went to until we got here."

"I'm not going in."

"Whatever. I am."

I heard the door close and opened my eyes to see Tess walking toward the building. It felt wrong on so many levels even to be here. But sitting in the car seemed kind of stupid, too. I probably wouldn't have been so upset about it if Liam had called after the food court debacle. It would look as if I had gone there for him when I was really only there for Tess.

But if that was the truth, then it shouldn't matter what Lexi thought, right?

It shouldn't, but it really, really did.

Then everything got so much worse. I looked up and saw Liam come out of one of the doors and slowly look around the parking lot. I slunk down into my seat, but he paused when he looked my way and then started walking to the car. A rush of desperation went through me. *Hide? Run? Hot-wire the car and drive away?*

He stood at my door looking down at me. I felt like a four-year-old.

Since I didn't have the keys to lower the window, my only choice was to get out of the car. Which I did. With as much of my pride intact as possible. It wasn't much.

"My sister goes here," I blurted out. *So much for my pride.*

"I'm glad you came. I wanted to apologize for . . . for what happened yesterday."

"You didn't do anything."

"I just didn't know what to do. Every time I say something, I feel like I screw up. I hate hurting people's feelings, and I didn't mean to lead anyone on. . . ."

I felt sick. Truly, truly sick. *He thinks he's leading me on?* "It's okay. You're not going to hurt my feelings. I have a boyfriend, anyway." It just slipped out.

"What?" Liam looked stunned. "We talked about this. You said—"

I cut him off. "Oh, we got back together this morning. So you don't have to worry about me."

Liam took a small but very definitive step backward, then turned and strode away.

I crawled back in the car, curled up, and sobbed until my head ached.

"What did you do?"

I jumped. Tess slammed the door shut. I wiped my face and smoothed my hair as I tried to get my bearings. I sat up, looked around the parking lot, and realized that the awful nightmare was all too real.

"I send Liam out here to get you, and he comes back and not only refuses to talk to me but skulks in a corner the entire time. What happened?"

"I told him I got back together with Todd."

"You *what?*" Tess grabbed my shoulders and shook me. "What is wrong with you? Todd is dead. Remember?"

"You don't understand. Liam was standing here telling me how he didn't want to hurt my feelings and that he felt bad for leading me on. . . ."

"You're an idiot, Mallory."

"But that's exactly what he said. He just felt sorry for—"

"He was talking about *Lexi*!! He felt bad for Lexi, and he was trying to find an easy way to let her down. He told me that right before I sent him out to the car! He likes you, and you go and resurrect Todd?" Tess covered her face with her hands and screamed and then got eerily silent for several minutes.

"You're going in there, and you're gonna tell him the truth before he has a chance to feel bad enough for Lexi to actually ask her out."

"The service is over, isn't it?"

"No. You have enough time to fix this."

"I can't."

"Yes, you can, Mallory. If you don't tell him, I will."

"You wouldn't."

Tess just raised that eyebrow. She would.

"I can't face any more humiliation."

"Then you shouldn't have raised Todd from the dead." Tess got out of the car and came around to my side. She yanked open my door. "Get out."

I obeyed. I followed her into the building, and she led me down several hallways to a large room in the back of the church. The room was full of teens, and everyone was milling around in small groups, talking and drinking from small red plastic cups.

Lexi and Liam were sitting in two metal folding chairs in a corner, talking. Tess pointed at them. I wished I could borrow some of her bravado, but it was my mess. I needed to fix it. *Step 5 again.*

But I had to make this confession. Not just to any human being, but to Liam. I could tell he was hurt, and I was to blame.

It was ironic that I was standing in a church. I didn't understand God, but at that moment I needed his help. And maybe, just maybe, God would come through for me.

I took a deep breath and walked toward them. They both stopped talking and looked at me. *Speak.*

"Liam, can I talk to you for a minute?"

He glanced at Lexi, who didn't seem happy. He shrugged and stood up. I led him as far away from everyone as I could, then turned to face him.

Liam's expression was unreadable. Other than the hurt. That was clear. Maybe anger, too.

"Okay, I kind of lied to you. I mean, I *did* lie. I thought you were telling me that you liked Lexi, and I guess I was embarrassed and wanted to make it look like it didn't matter to me, even though it did. So I lied and said I got back together with my boyfriend, which isn't true; but it was the only thing I could think of to make it seem like I was okay with you going out with Lexi, because I am totally not okay with that, and I'm kind of hoping you might give me another chance."

Liam looked a little confused. *Is he just processing? Oh, God. What if he doesn't believe me?* That's when I made the incredibly stupid decision to keep talking.

"I mean, to be completely honest, I never even had a boyfriend. I made him up. I didn't want to be the only person who was a virgin, so I pretended I had this boyfriend and told everyone we had sex, even though he wasn't real and I'm still a virgin and I'm not the same person inside that I pretend to be at school, and I just thought you should know that before you decide to go out with Lexi."

As soon as I stopped talking, I wanted to run from the room. But I couldn't convince the muscles in my legs to move. They were like stone pillars beneath me, forcing me to witness waves of indefinable emotion cross Liam's face.

He reached down, took my hand, and led me out of the room and into the hallway. "Let me get this straight. You didn't get back together with your boyfriend?"

"No."

"You just said that because you were jealous of Lexi?"

"I didn't say I was jealous of . . . yes."

A grin spread across Liam's face. "I'm so glad to hear that."

"What? That I'm a compulsive liar?"

Liam shrugged and squeezed my hand. "You came and told me the truth. That took guts."

"I guess." As he looked at me, the humiliation and fear and nerves started to melt away, and I got swept up again in those brown eyes.

He leaned close, then kissed me gently on the cheek.

"Are you allowed to do that in church?"

He kissed me again. "Probably not."

The halls around us started to fill up as people began to leave. Tess walked over and planted herself right next to us.

"Are you two fixed?"

Liam laughed. "Yes, Tess. We'll be fine."

"Finally," she said as she walked away.

"I still think I need to hear that whole story. It's all a little confusing right now," Liam said. "But it sounds pretty amazing."

"Which part?"

"That you went to such elaborate lengths to hide being a virgin."

I didn't get why *that* impressed him, but at that moment I didn't really care. *Liam likes me!*

"I know things keep getting messed up, but I don't want to give up on . . . this."

"I don't either," I said.

He pulled me close, wrapped his arms around me, and squeezed. So many emotions washed through me that I couldn't have sorted them out if I tried. He ended the hug far too soon and smiled at me. "Want to get some lunch? It's a group thing, so you can bring Tess."

"Is Lexi coming?"

He gave a deep sigh. "Probably. But you're gonna have to get used to her if you're going to hang around me. She is a friend, and she kind of comes with all of this." He gestured vaguely around him.

"I suppose I can live with that. But she hates me."

"She doesn't hate you. Look, I'll talk to her."

"Will you do it soon? The death stares are kind of freaking me out."

"Promise."

He agreed to drive Tess and I home, so I went to find her and Darby. Darby was actually glad we had found a ride since she wanted to go out to lunch with friends, too.

I finally found Tess sitting in a café in the church lobby with a guy who looked a bit older. He was cute, with reddish hair and a smattering of freckles across his face. They looked deeply engaged in conversation, so I positioned myself nearby and tried to get her attention. She glanced up and waved me over.

"This is my friend, Mallory. Mallory, this is Rick Wesley. He's the youth pastor here."

Rick stood up and shook my hand. "Actually, I'm just an intern. I'm glad you guys came today."

"Thanks."

We all stood silently (read: awkwardly) for a few seconds, then Rick excused himself to talk to someone else. I quickly filled in Tess on Liam and the group lunch I had agreed to.

She cringed. "You actually told him that Todd was a fake? Wow. I just wanted you to tell him that you didn't get back together with him."

"It all came tumbling out. I couldn't stop myself. But you know, I'm kind of glad. I feel so much better!" I grabbed her in a hug. "Thank you, Tess. You're the best."

"I know." She smirked.

CHAPTER 9

If Liam had told me that the "group lunch" would be every person in his teen group crammed into the back room of Shoney's, I might have said no. Even being near Liam didn't help the situation.

For one, I was starting to regret that I had confessed my most precious secret to a guy I hardly knew. What was to stop him from mentioning it to someone else? I knew that was all it would take to get it effectively dispersed throughout North County High. And two, I didn't really know anybody. Small talk wasn't one of my best skills, and the few people I did talk to managed to bring up God within seconds.

"So what is your relationship with the Lord?"

"How can I be praying for you?"

"Have you made a commitment to Jesus Christ?"

Egads! I probably ate two full breakfasts, what with stuffing food in my mouth every few minutes to avoid answering questions. Seriously. How was I supposed to know the answer to any of those things?

Tess, for her part, looked as if she belonged there, chatting with several different people—even several guys— as comfortably as ever. I wondered how she was answering all the questions. And Liam, the new guy in town, seemed to know just about everyone. But he never left my side, so he scored major points for that.

But if being around Liam meant being around all of these other people . . . I just didn't know how I felt about it. It was intimidating. Lexi was there with a couple of other people from school whom I recognized, but most of the kids were new to me. I felt out of place, and I wasn't completely sure why.

Liam drove Tess and I back to my house. As soon as we pulled in the driveway, Tess waved and bolted from the car, leaving Liam and me alone.

Liam laughed. "I'm glad you came today, really glad. If you come earlier next time, you'll get to see me play."

"Next time?"

"Yeah. You're coming back, right?"

I looked down and twirled the ring around my finger. "I don't know."

"It can be overwhelming at first. Don't give up on it too easily."

I looked back at him, at his smile, at his soft brown eyes, and I got really, really nervous. If I didn't fit into his church life, maybe I wouldn't fit into his life at all. And I desperately wanted to.

He picked up my hand and kissed it, then brushed his other hand across my cheek. "You have no idea how glad I was to hear about your pretend boyfriend."

"I was expecting you to be mad."

"No way. It's a huge relief. I mean, it puts us on a level playing field. I thought maybe, with who you were—knowing so many people, being a cheerleader—I thought I might be getting in over my head. But now I can relax."

I stiffened. "Because, of course, cheerleaders automatically sleep around."

"No. That's not what I meant."

"But you made the assumption."

"I guess I did. I was wrong. So wrong. Monstrously wrong. Can you ever forgive me?"

I let a smile slip out. He was so cute! "I suppose."

"Good. Then I'll see you tomorrow. Oh, wait." He took out his cell phone and pointed it at me. "There, now I can see your face when you call me."

"Nice. You could've given me a little warning."

"Nah, it's more fun this way. I'll talk to you later. And I still want to hear that whole story."

I got another kiss on the cheek; and even though I wanted him to kiss me for real, I was okay with it. Slow was better. Slow would keep me from getting scared and running off.

Tess was pacing my room with her cell phone to her ear when I got inside.

"Yes, I'll be there. Soon. I've got it, Ash. All right. Bye." Tess snapped the phone closed.

"What?" I asked.

"Ashley's home, and Mom's not there, and she's flipping out on me. I've got to go."

"Will you call me later? Or come by?"

"I'll try." She grabbed her bag and slung it over her shoulder. *"Hasta."*

After she left I sat at my computer and fiddled around with the fund-raiser poster while replaying the day in my head.

I should have been giddy with excitement. Instead I felt paralyzed. As if it were all a nice dream that would slip away when I woke up. It was all too good to be true. Wasn't it?

I dragged myself to school the next morning determined to find Tess. Her phone had gone to voice mail, and I hadn't heard from her all night. But it was Liam I found first. He was leaning against my locker, his hands in his pockets and a sheepish grin on his face. I felt a sudden rush of excitement. For years I had dreamed of someone waiting by my locker for me. Dating an invisible guy long-distance had made the locker thing kind of impossible.

I slowed my walk just to take in the sight. *An actual guy, waiting for me.* I was in heaven.

"Morning." He yawned. "I can't seem to wake up today."

"Me neither." I opened my locker, and Liam leaned in over my shoulder. He was so close I could smell him.

"What'cha got in here?"

He glanced around my locker. A mirror on the door, pictures of Tess and me and ones with Yvie and Sophie, other cheerleaders. He picked up my bobblehead hula monkey from the top shelf.

"Now this is different."

I snatched it from him. "Leave my monkey alone." I placed it back on the shelf. "Tess gave him to me when we were in third grade and I was going through my monkey phase."

Liam shook his head. "I wouldn't even know what that's like. Having the same friend for years." He leaned his back up against the next locker, and his face took on a melancholy look.

"You don't keep in touch with people?"

"I try, but it doesn't last. Once you move on, it either

becomes a Facebook-level friendship or they forget all about you."

I closed my locker and moved in front of him. "I would think you'd be pretty hard to forget."

"You'd think, wouldn't you?" He laughed. "I just see you and Tess and think how different my life would be if my dad did something else."

"Speaking of Tess, I need to go find her. I'll see you at lunch, okay?"

"Sure." He grabbed my hand and squeezed it, then waved as he walked away. I turned to go in the opposite direction and ran straight into Lexi.

I gave a heavy sigh but refrained from rolling my eyes.

"Do you have a minute?" she asked.

"Not really."

"I know what you're doing."

Apparently it didn't matter what I said.

"And what is it I'm doing, Lexi?"

"I can't believe you'd show up at church. Just to go out with some guy. That's low. Even for someone like you."

I could have defended myself, but it didn't matter. I had less than four minutes to find Tess before the bell rang.

I walked past her, realizing that she was not going to back off despite Liam's far-fetched hopes.

"This isn't over," Lexi called out, her words getting swallowed in the noise of the hallway.

What could she do to me, anyway?

"Tess! I've been looking for you everywhere." I found her at her locker when I went back to check for a third time.

"I'm so late!" Tess looked frazzled.

"Are you okay? You never answered your phone. I was worried."

"I know. I'm sorry. I'll tell you at lunch. I'm fine, but now we're both going to be late."

The bell rang loudly, and we sprinted away. She was here, and that's all I needed to know.

I spent the first part of the day avoiding Lexi. I wasn't scared of her; I just didn't feel like dealing with her. She shot daggers at me during PE. Even Katie noticed.

"What did you do to her?" she asked.

"We like the same guy."

Katie laughed, then stopped. "Wait. You're serious? You two don't seem like you'd go for the same type of guy. At all." Katie lined up her arrow and let it fly, hitting the target dead center.

And when I thought about it, it did seem strange. But when I was all occupied with Todd, I never had the chance to see what kind of guy I liked. Now I knew. Did that make me like Lexi? I shuddered.

On the way to lunch I spotted Lexi talking with Liam in the lobby. I slowed, trying to decide whether or not I should approach. Liam and I were sort of together, so I felt as if I could, but I wanted to look secure, even if I didn't feel that way. He glanced up at me, smiled, said something to Lexi, then walked over and joined me. Problem solved.

"Hey, you."

"Hey." I fell into step beside him, and he slung an arm over my shoulder. He was taller than me, so I felt all tucked in and safe. A rush of warmth went through me. *So this is how it feels.*

When we got inside, Tess was standing near the lunch line waiting for me. I was still a little concerned about her and wasn't sure what to do with Liam. I didn't want to boot him to another table, especially with Lexi hovering around. But Tess needed me.

Liam noticed. "You okay?" he asked.

"Sure. It's just that Tess is . . ."

"Do you want to eat with Tess?" he asked.

I hesitated. "Do you mind? She's got some stuff going on in her life right now and . . ."

"I don't mind. I'll catch up with you later, okay?"

I wanted to tell him how amazing he was, but all that came out was "Thanks."

I went over and joined Tess.

"You didn't have to get rid of him," Tess said.

"Yes, I did."

We got our lunch and found a table by a window, far enough away to hear each other but not so far away that we could be overheard.

"So spill it."

"It's all fine now. Mom went down to the station to try and bail out Darren, but they're holding him. She threw a big stink and ended up staying there overnight, so I had to pick her up this morning and get her home." Tess shook her head. "She's completely out of control."

"What will you do?"

Tess pushed the food around on her plate, looking

defeated. "Maintain the status quo. I'm just worried about Ash telling someone. She's worn out her welcome at her friend's house, so I need to find another place for her to go, or I guess I just need to stay home with her."

"Tess."

"Don't go there, Mall. I'm not telling anyone."

"Could foster care be any worse than what's already going on?"

"Yes." She fell quiet, eating a few bites of food. Her eyes were red and rimmed with tears, and I felt so completely helpless. But I was also surer than ever that, at this rate, they wouldn't make it eighteen more months.

"Then I'm staying at your house this coming weekend. We'll both take care of Ashley."

Tess smiled sadly and shook her head.

"Tess, I'm not letting you deal with this alone."

"You have no idea what it's like, Mallory. Trust me. You don't want to be there."

"I do. I can handle it."

"Let's just see how the week goes, okay?"

"Okay."

"Now." Tess shook her curls and sat up a little straighter. "What's going on with Liam?"

I filled her in on our short conversations and my run-in with Lexi.

"Man, that girl's got nerve."

"Yeah, but Liam doesn't seem worried about her."

Tess shrugged. "Don't let your guard down around her. Oh, and remember that youth pastor guy, Rick? He called me last night."

"No way."

"Yeah. I made some random comment about my mom being psycho, and he said he wanted to make sure I was okay." Tess shrugged again.

"You should tell him about your mom. He doesn't have to report what you say."

Tess considered this. "Are you sure?"

"Yeah. Darby told me about that once. Unless you're threatening to hurt someone else or yourself, they can keep everything you say confidential."

Tess seemed to consider this, and it gave me some hope. Maybe he would talk her into getting real help.

I stopped by my locker after school and found Liam waiting there again. Twice in one day.

"Can I take you home after practice?" he asked.

"You want to wait that long? We usually don't get finished till four thirty, sometimes later."

"I'm staying, anyway. I'm helping out with an assembly with some kids from my church."

My stomach fell. Lexi would be there. "Okay. Well, if you don't mind waiting."

"I don't." He leaned down and kissed me on the cheek but lingered, pressing his cheek against mine. "I love the way your hair smells." Then he stepped back and was gone.

I trudged to practice and tossed my stuff in my locker.

"What's with the scowl?" Tess asked.

"Lexi." I told Tess about Liam's project.

Tess snorted. "He likes you, Mallory. I wouldn't worry about it. Of course, I still think I need to have another talk with her."

"Oh, no, you don't. I'll deal with Lexi." But I knew that I wouldn't say anything to her unless forced to.

I had already won.

That was enough, wasn't it?

CHAPTER 10

Practice was extra long because we were learning a new dance routine for homecoming. I really was trying to learn the steps, but I kept staring at the clock, wondering how much alone time I was giving Lexi and Liam.

Tess wagged her finger at me. "Quit stressing."

And I wanted to, oh, how I wanted to. But having a pretend boyfriend in no way prepared me for the feelings of insecurity and outright jealousy that were flying through me. Lexi wasn't going to go away, though. She came with the territory. I'd have to get used to it or, well, I didn't really want to think about the alternative. I wanted to have a chance with Liam.

Finally Tara told us we could go home. I took a quick shower and told Tess I'd be over later. Then I went looking for Liam.

I heard him long before I saw him. The music from a guitar echoed through the hallways. I turned the corner, and he was sitting by himself in the lobby, strumming the guitar. I stopped and watched him, his full concentration on the instrument in his hands. Light streamed in through the window behind him. I wasn't that into music, but the song sounded beautiful.

He looked up and placed his hand across the strings to stop the sound.

"Don't stop. That was amazing." I walked over and sat beside him, dropping my bag on the floor. "Keep playing."

He looked at me sweetly, then began strumming again.

The music wrapped around us and then he began to sing.

"I have been to California,
and flown across the sea.
I've lived through New England winters
and melted in the South.
I've seen more beauty in this land
than I ever wished to see;
but sitting right here next to you,
well, there's nowhere I'd rather be."

I swear my heart stopped beating. He looked at me with a goofy smile.

"Wow. I've never heard that song. I love it," I said. I didn't tell him that the melody would be caught in my thoughts for a very long time.

"Of course you've never heard it. I've been writing it for you."

Again with the stopped heart. "For me?" I choked out.

He nodded. "That's all I have right now, though. It's a work in progress."

I stared at him, but there wasn't even a hint of humor on his face.

Pretend boyfriends also don't write songs and sing them to you in the lobby of your school.

How was I supposed to respond to something like that? I couldn't muster words, so I leaned over to kiss him on the cheek—but he turned and caught my lips with his. A real, honest-to-goodness kiss—soft, sweet, but too swift. He pulled back and cringed.

"Sorry 'bout that."

The warm glow inside me burned and crept up my cheeks. I dropped my head. Was I the bad influence Lexi accused me of being? *Why doesn't he want to kiss me?*

Liam lifted my chin and looked into my eyes. "Mallory, don't disappear on me. What's wrong?"

If he likes me so much, why does he keep rejecting me?

Liam sighed and looked at the ceiling. "Girls need to come with a special manual."

I wasn't sure if he was talking to me or not.

He shifted on the bench and took my hand. "Forget I did that, okay? I just want to be careful, for both our sakes."

"I wasn't trying . . ."

"No. No. Of course you weren't. I just really like you. I want to kiss you, believe me. But let's put it this way: I have very little self-control, so I try to avoid situations where I could be . . . impulsive."

And he thinks I'm hard to figure out. "I was just trying to thank you for the song."

"You're welcome."

I decided to shift the conversation. "So, is this your routine?"

"My routine?"

"Writing songs for girls."

"I'll never tell."

I shoved him playfully. "Come on. I should know what kind of competition I've got."

"You don't have any. I promise."

I wasn't so sure about that, but in the moment, I was willing to accept it. Liam gathered up his things and placed his guitar in its case.

"So where to?" he asked.

"Tess's."

I gave him basic directions as we walked to his car. It was just a small, two-door hatchback, but it was neat as a pin inside. For someone who ate garbage, he seemed to keep it out of his car.

On the way to Tess's house, Liam said, "Okay, I hate doing this kind of stuff, but Alex wanted to know if you thought Tess would say yes if he asked her to homecoming."

"No way. Tell him he can go with Cammie."

"Cammie?"

"Why do you hang out with him, anyway? He's kind of a jerk."

"He's lost."

I looked over at Liam, whose eyes were on the road.

"Lost, like, going-to-hell lost?"

"Well, I wouldn't put it that way. Alex can't help the way he is."

I scoffed.

"You don't agree, huh?"

I shrugged. "Turn left here. I don't know. I think we all make our own choices and can't blame the consequences on anybody but ourselves." I should know.

"I like Alex. I mean, I know he hurt your friend, but just because we've messed up doesn't mean that we shouldn't get the chance to make it right."

He had me there. "It's that one, with the red door," I said.

Liam pulled up to the curb and shut off the car. He shifted toward me. "So tell me your story."

I rolled my eyes. "It's not worth the energy it would take to tell it."

"C'mon. I want to know."

"The simple version is that all my friends started sleeping with their boyfriends, and I was the last virgin in the group and didn't want to be. So I made up Todd and told everyone I slept with him. End of story."

"Why didn't you want to have sex?"

I pulled at my long-sleeved shirt, feeling itchy and hot all of a sudden. Only having this conversation with my dad would make me more uncomfortable.

I narrowed my eyes at him. "Doing a report on me?"

"I'm genuinely interested. I just want to know why."

"Because I wasn't ready to." Not the complete truth, but enough. "So fair's fair. Tell me something I don't know about you."

Liam leaned back in his seat and drummed his fingers on the steering wheel—and got very quiet.

"What is it?" I had never seen Liam with that sad expression before.

He turned to me and shrugged. "Things at home, they're kind of tough."

I could relate to that. I waited for him to continue.

"It's just, I thought moving here would be so great, and being with my brother—he lives close by—has been awesome. But my dad . . . you don't want to hear all this."

"I do." I reached over and rested my hand on his arm. He smiled weakly and put his hand on top of mine.

"My dad expected both Brian and me to go into the military. He was furious when Brian decided to go to medical school instead. He cut him off financially and told Brian that if he was going to turn down a free ride, he wasn't about to give him one. So now being near Brian has been great and horrible at the same time 'cause Dad can't let it go."

"What about your mom?"

"She just wants everyone to get along and love one another." Liam shook his head. "I thought Dad would ease up once he saw how great Brian was doing."

"I'm so sorry, Liam."

"It's not your fault. It's not even mine. But Dad is so fixated on Brian's decision that he's pressuring me to decide what branch I want to go into."

"Do you want to?"

Liam got quiet again and took several slow, deep breaths. Finally he said, "I don't know."

I felt like I did with Tess. Helpless.

But then I considered the little I knew about Liam. "Guess they don't have many music programs at military schools, huh?"

"Not the kind that I'm interested in. Dad thinks the music I like is a silly hobby. 'What kind of moron thinks playing for his country isn't good enough?' He doesn't get it. If it wasn't for my mom, music lessons would never have happened."

I glanced over at Tess's house. I knew I should go in, but I wanted to stay with Liam, too. It was the closest I had ever felt to any guy. "So what will you do?"

"I have no idea. But I'm certainly not gonna figure it out today. Go see Tess. It's okay." He smiled at me and brought my hand to his mouth and kissed it. "You know. You're the first person I've told that to."

"Not even your friends at church?"

"Not even them."

I leaned over and kissed him on the cheek and then climbed out of the car, my heart feeling both full and sad at the same time.

Tess was at the door when I got there. She looked me up and down, taking me in, reading my body language. She crossed her arms. "You okay?" she asked.

"I *really* like him."

She grinned and threw her arms around me, but a loud crash from inside the house stopped us cold. Tess bolted inside, leaving the door wide-open. I stepped through, knowing that there was no turning back.

I wandered down the hallway toward the sound of sobbing. Tess was standing over her mom in the bathroom, broken glass around them and bright-red blood on the mirror, sink, and floor.

"Get a towel from the closet. Behind you," Tess said.

I pulled open the closet. Ashley slipped in beside me and grabbed a dark-blue towel from the shelf.

"Use this one," she said quietly. Ashley tucked her blond hair behind her ears and stuffed her hands into her pockets. She glanced in the bathroom.

"Go to your room, Ashley. I've got this," Tess said.

Mrs. Howard kept sobbing. She reeked of alcohol, and she was dirty. It was hard to tell how hurt she was. Tess tried to get her mom's hand under the running water in the sink, but her mother refused to stand. She was just dead weight on the floor.

"This is all your fault," Mrs. Howard cried.

"Yep. All mine. Mallory, grab one side and push. We'll use the tub."

Between us, we pushed her toward the bathtub, trying to move the bigger chunks of glass out of the way. Tess ran the water and got her mom's hand underneath. The cuts seemed small except for a big one across her palm.

"Does she need stitches?" I asked.

"Probably." Tess put her hand on her forehead. "I can't take her to the hospital like this."

"Why do you hate me?" Mrs. Howard yelled.

"I don't hate you." Tess spoke quietly, as if she had said it a million times before.

Tess pulled back the towel to look at the palm again, and blood oozed out. She covered it quickly and squeezed.

"We'll just have to bandage it up. Here, hold this." Tess gave me her mom's hand and the towel, and Mrs. Howard rolled a little, her head wrapped in her other arm. She kept sobbing. Tess stood and yanked open the medicine cabinet.

"It could get infected. And it's on her palm. If it's not stitched up right, it'll scar and she won't be able to use that hand right."

Tess turned up her mom's palm and poured hydrogen peroxide over it.

Mrs. Howard screamed. "Stop it! Stop it! You're killing me!" She thrashed her arms around.

"Grab her arms. Keep her still," Tess yelled to me above her mom's screams.

"I'm *trying*."

For someone so slight, her mom was super strong. It took everything I had to keep her down, and she still managed to get me in the jaw with her elbow. But the pain in my face was nothing compared to what I felt inside watching Tess.

Then I got an idea. "Liam's brother. He's in medical school."

"He's still in school?"

"Yeah. But he'd know how to do stitches, wouldn't he?"

Tess frowned. "Would he come?"

"I don't know. But it's worth a shot."

"No. No. We can't risk it. He'll tell. He'll have to. No. We'll wrap it up really good and hope for the best."

"Tess. Be reasonable! We have to . . ."

"There is no reason to any of this, Mallory. There never was. You can help me, but you can't judge me."

"I'm not judging you!"

"Yes, you are. You think I can't handle this."

"I know you can handle it. You can handle anything. But you shouldn't *have* to. Tess, look around. This is not okay."

Tess grew quiet. Mrs. Howard had become silent, too, except for an occasional soft snore. Tess stepped over her mom and left the room, returning a minute later with a broom and dustpan, tears streaming down her face.

"I'm sorry, Tess."

I picked up the larger pieces of mirror while Tess swept up the smaller shards.

"You just don't understand," Tess said, almost under her breath.

"No, I don't. But I also know you can't do this alone." I paused, weighing my next words carefully, knowing how Tess would react. "What about your dad, Tess?"

"Not an option." She kept sweeping.

"But if he knew what was happening . . ."

She looked up, the tears still flowing. "He does know. And he doesn't care."

"What?"

"I called him. And I quote, 'She's not my problem anymore.'"

"But what about you and Ashley?"

Tess shrugged and looked down at her mom.

Tess's dad had taken off when Tess was eight—in third grade. I had met him once. Honestly, it was probably why we were as close as sisters. We'd spent that whole year together. Me delighting in a new friend, her simply trying to cope with the pain. Over the years she had talked to him occasionally, and it had always put Tess in a terrible mood for days. Last I had heard he lived in another state with a brand-new family. I was almost as surprised by her calling him as I was to hear that he felt that it wasn't his concern. Anger curled up inside me like a thick red rope. If he had been in the room, I would have strangled him and felt no remorse.

Together we moved Mrs. Howard into her bedroom to sleep it off. Tess left to go check on Ashley, and I went back to the bathroom to finish cleaning up the glass and the blood. I scrubbed the floor and the sink, and picked out the large pieces of glass that were still stuck to the mirror frame. I caught sight of my broken reflection and stared at it. *What am I supposed to do?*

I didn't know the answer, but I was pretty sure I was in over my head. It was one of those God-sized problems that Darby had talked about.

I wasn't much of a pray-er. Wasn't even totally sure how to do it. But I dropped my head. *Help us. Please.*

I turned to see Tess standing in the doorway. "I think you need to call Liam."

CHAPTER 11

Tess hovered close by, antsy and nervous, giving instructions.

"Tell him he has to come here. And make sure he's not going to say anything. Tell him that she can't go to the hospital because she's deathly afraid to go."

I glared at Tess. "Will you let me handle this?"

She turned away and dropped onto the couch, putting her hands over her face.

"You still there?" I asked.

"Yeah. But I'm not sure I get it," Liam said.

"Sorry. I just need to know if you think Brian would come over to Tess's house and stitch up her mom's hand."

"Why doesn't she just go to the emergency room?"

"If it were that simple I wouldn't be calling."

"And you're not going to give me anything else?"

"Liam, please. It's important. Her mom is too scared to go, and she needs her hand stitched up."

"I don't know if he'll do it."

"Convince him. Please?"

"I'll call you back."

I ended the call and went to sit next to Tess, but she jumped up as soon as I sat and started cleaning the living room. I joined her, grabbing empty liquor bottles and stacking papers neatly. I pulled open the shades. The sun was starting to set, but it still made a huge improvement to the room.

My phone rang twice; but both times it was Darby, and I just let it go to voice mail. I didn't want to miss Liam's call. Tess hurried around cleaning; and when the living room was straight, she started in on the kitchen. She threw a frozen pizza in the oven and tore open a package of cookies, the kind you break apart and bake.

"Cookies?" I asked.

"The smell of fresh-baked cookies gives the illusion of normalcy." Tess placed the doughy squares on the cookie sheet.

"Is it like this all the time?" I asked.

"Some days are better, some are worse. This Darren thing has definitely made things worse."

My phone rang. It was Liam.

"He'll come over, but he's not happy about it. We'll be there soon."

"Thank you, Liam. Thank you so much."

I closed the phone. "They're on their way."

Tess blew out her breath. "I'm going to go check on her. See if I can get her up and out here."

"Do you want help?"

Tess shook her head and walked down the hallway.

I sat on the couch to wait. Within minutes there was a knock at the door. But instead of Liam and his brother, I found Darby standing there, a grin on her face.

"I knew you'd be here. I've got to talk to you and Tess," Darby said.

"It's not a good time."

Darby's face grew serious. "What's wrong? Mallory?"

I tried to swallow my tears. Seeing her standing there just made me want to fall into her arms. I wanted her to tell me that everything was going to be okay. I brushed at the one tear that escaped. Mom would *kill* me if I got Darby involved in this.

"Nothing. It's fine. Maybe we can get together tomorrow."

Darby put one hand on her hip. "Look at me, Mallory. Do I seem unstable or depressed to you?"

"No."

"Then quit trying to protect me. I want to help."

"I know you do, but . . ." I couldn't tell her that "protecting her" was practically in Mom's job description for me.

Just behind her I saw Liam's car pull into the driveway. An older version of Liam climbed out the passenger side. Brian carried a bag and walked toward the porch.

He stopped in front of Darby. He was a head taller than she was, and he was staring at her.

"Don't I know you?" he asked.

"Church, I think. You go to Riverside Fellowship, right?"

Brian snapped his finger. "That's it," he said. "I'm Brian Crawford." He still hadn't so much as acknowledged me.

"Darby Dane." They shook hands, smiling at each other. Liam came over and squeezed my hand.

"So what's going on here?" Brian asked.

"I have no idea. This is my sister, Mallory."

Brian looked at me. "I'm not sure this is the wisest thing to do. I'll take a look but . . ."

"It'll probably be a snap for you." I pulled open the door, and everyone crowded into the small living room. Darby came in, too, even though I gave her a look begging her to go home.

"I'll go get Tess." I hurried down the hallway and pushed open the door.

"I can't get her up." Tess was distraught. "They can't come back here."

I glanced around the room; evidence of her mother's bender was everywhere.

"You get on one side, and I'll get on the other."

We pulled Mrs. Howard upright. She moaned but didn't say anything. Fortunately, she wasn't very big, so we were able to get her to her feet and move her toward the doorway. But since the hallway was only big enough for two people, we had to turn sideways and shuffle ourselves down the hall to the living room.

"Whadya think you're doin'?" her mom slurred.

"You need to see a doctor. Your hand is cut," Tess said.

"Whaa?" Mrs. Howard looked at her hand and the thick towel knotted around it.

As soon as we came into the living room, Brian and Liam jumped in and took Mrs. Howard from us and walked her to the couch. When they set her down, Mrs. Howard flopped like a rag doll, unable even to lift her head.

"Who are you?" she asked.

"I'm Brian Crawford. I'm just going to take a look at your hand."

Brian was amazing with Mrs. Howard. He spoke in a soft, gentle voice, explaining everything he was doing. Mrs. Howard didn't argue. She seemed confused about the whole thing. Darby pulled me over into a corner.

"She's wasted," Darby said.

I shrugged.

"Mallory. Is she taking care of Tess and her sister?"

"Please stay out of it, Darby. Go home. It'll be fine."

Mrs. Howard yelled out from the couch, but Brian

calmed her back down. I went and stood beside Liam. "Your brother is a saint," I said.

Liam laughed. "Don't let him hear you say that. I'll never hear the end of it."

"Is this going to cause problems for you?"

Liam shook his head and squeezed my hand. "He doesn't mind helping at all. I think he's just worried about getting into trouble."

"I think it's best for all of us if we don't mention this to anyone, anyway."

Brian finished with her hand, and Mrs. Howard promptly fell back asleep.

Brian stood up and looked at Tess. "Can I talk to you for a minute?"

Tess nodded and followed him into the kitchen. I walked back over to Darby.

"Why did you come here?" I asked.

Darby knowing about Tess created that much more pressure for me. For both of us.

"The warehouse. We've got one. I wanted to tell you and Tess."

"Look, Darby. You have to forget all this, okay?"

"Mallory."

"It's Tess's choice, and she doesn't want anyone to say anything. You can understand that, can't you?" It was a bit of a dig, but I was desperate.

She dropped her chin and nodded.

"C'mon, Liam." Brian came out of the kitchen and strode out the door, followed by Darby. Liam squeezed my shoulder and gave me a sympathetic smile but hurried out after them. I found Tess sitting at the table, her head buried in her arms.

"Tess?"

She looked up, her eyes red and puffy.

"Is Brian going to . . . ?"

Tess shook her head. "I don't think so, but he's upset about it."

"Yeah, Darby wasn't happy either."

"Why did you let her in here?" Tess's words were sharp.

"I . . . I didn't mean to. They all showed up at the same time."

"That's just great." Tess pushed away from the table. She began scrubbing the counters hard and tossing items toward the sink.

"Tess, I'm sorry. Darby came to tell us we have a place for the toy drive."

Tess's movements slowed and then she turned and nodded. "Good. Good. Then we can finish the posters, start letting people know. . . ." Tess rambled on about the toy drive, making plans, taking on the role of the confident committee leader.

What else could I do but let her?

CHAPTER 12

I got up extra early on Tuesday so that I could go home and shower before school. Tess was still sleeping, so my only option was walking. I scribbled a note for her to pick me up and set out for home.

I could do the walk in my sleep, which was a good thing since I had tossed and turned most of the night. I kept having dreams about Darren breaking in and killing us all as we slept. I knew it was ridiculous. Darren was in the county jail, but it was still scary. Every little noise made me jump.

As soon as I walked into the house, Darby pounced.

"What's going on, Mallory?" Darby stepped in front of the stairs, blocking my path to a hot shower.

"I told you last night—I need you to stay out of it."

"I can't. If you're going to spend the night in that house, Mom needs to know. *Someone* needs to know about it."

"Who?" I filled Darby in on every excuse Tess had given me. "There's nothing you can do."

Darby frowned. "She needs help, Mallory. You have to see that."

I pushed past her, frustrated with how much I agreed with her and how little that mattered. I had to help Tess get through the next eighteen months. That was my mission. Along with seeing if I could snag Liam as a boyfriend. I could totally do both.

I showered and changed quickly but got cornered by my mom in the kitchen.

"Did you see Darby this morning?" Mom was still packing her bags for school.

"Yeah." The less I said, the better.

"Did she look okay to you? She's upset but won't talk about it." Mom pressed her fingers to her lips. "What do you think's wrong? Maybe I should call in sick and stay here."

I could almost feel that dark cloud of worry moving back over the house. Darby was upset, but I didn't think it was the level of upset that Mom was thinking. But what did I know? None of us had thought she would do what she did. Something like that forever changes the realm of what is possible.

But I still said, "I think she's okay."

Mom looked at her watch and shook her head. "I have to go. Keep a close eye on her, and see if you can find out what's going on, okay?"

I nodded, feeling uneasy about how all this fell on me.

Mom hurried off, and Tess was waiting outside when I came out. She grinned, an obvious clue that we weren't going to talk about moms this morning. Which was just fine with me.

"So, does Darby really have a place for us?"

I handed Tess the sheet of paper Darby had given me. "We need to go over and sign something at the leasing office to make it official. But there's a problem."

"What?"

"Darby's really upset about last night. I may not be able to stop her from saying something to my parents."

Tess's eyes grew dark. "You have to. There's no room for mistakes."

"Last night was a huge mistake then, because now we have three more people who know."

"Brian promised not to say anything. And you can manage Liam and Darby."

Sure. Simple.

Normally, I'd be looking forward to B Day, but even having Liam waiting at my locker didn't help.

"Brian's ticked with me." Liam wrapped his arms around me and squeezed.

"Sorry about that. He's not going to say anything, though, right?" I hung up my jacket and grabbed my books.

"I don't think so."

"You have to know for sure, Liam. You have no idea how important it is."

"But, Mallory, she can't handle that by herself. . . ."

"You, too? You don't think I've already tried? Look, it's her decision—not yours or anybody else's." I slammed my locker. "Got it?"

Liam lifted his hands like I was holding a gun to his chest. "Got it."

The bell rang.

"I'm sorry. I'm just tired."

He kissed me on the cheek and left for class while I trudged in the opposite direction. Protecting Tess was quickly becoming a full-time job.

The week dragged by. Tess didn't stay overnight and wouldn't let me stay at her house, despite some begging on my part. I was worried, but Tess wouldn't talk about it.

Things were going well with Liam, and if I ignored the Lexi death stare I got every time she saw me, I was feeling pretty good about the relationship. He'd show up between classes, take my hand, and even drop notes into my locker. I was in both heaven and hell at the same time.

My dad agreed to be our photographer. He even seemed excited about it. So the fund-raiser was shaping up, which made Tess appear happy and content. I knew it was all just a front.

I had been looking forward to Friday all week, because not only did we have a pep rally and game (which was always a nice distraction), but we even had an assembly scheduled for first period. What could be better than a day without PE?

I joined the streams of kids headed into the auditorium, trying to spot Tess's curls in the crowd. She waved, and I slowly made my way toward her. I reached her before I could find Liam in the crowd.

Tess had her notebook out, and we immediately started whispering about fund-raiser details. Assemblies were a great time to catch up on things. I wasn't even totally sure what this one was about, except that it was the first of four scheduled for the school's "Safe Homecoming" campaign. One was always about drunk driving, which I wouldn't do even if I had a car, and there was usually one on sex. For some people, homecoming was a time to try and have sex at school without getting caught.

Principal Rodgers, who was five-foot-nothing but could scare the crap out of you when necessary, climbed up to the lectern. The noise level dropped noticeably.

"Ladies and gentleman—and I use those terms very loosely—you will give your full attention to Barbara Whittiker. She is the founder of Debating on Waiting."

A snicker rippled through the audience.

Principal Rodgers pointed at us. "And you will be respectful and listen or there will be no homecoming."

We all quieted down. I seriously doubted that Rodgers could take away homecoming but, like everyone else seemed to think, *Why risk it?*

Tess and I hunkered down and used hand signals to talk through our plans. I didn't hear much of anything until one line caught my attention. "Would you lie about your sex life just to impress your friends?"

My head snapped up.

"Suppose all your friends were talking about sex. Suppose they tried to make you feel stupid and naive for being a virgin. Would you go ahead and have sex, or would you maybe choose to lie about it?"

Tess looked up, too. "Where is she going with this?"

I shushed her, my eyes fixed on the speaker. Panic rose up my throat, making it difficult to breathe. *Relax, it means nothing. She couldn't possible know anything.*

"I heard a story just the other day that may shock you. It's about a beautiful, popular girl, a cheerleader, who is a virgin."

Laughter erupted all around, but Tess reached over and squeezed my hand.

"Now wait." The speaker held up her hands, but the laughter continued until Principal Rodgers stood up from her front-row seat and glared at everyone.

"This girl decided that instead of admitting that she

didn't want to have sex, she'd lie about it. She decided to tell her friends that she was having sex with her long-distance boyfriend."

The laughter and whispers grew louder. And every head that turned in my direction seemed to be looking at my guilty face. I slid farther down into the seat.

The speaker paused, waiting for a break in the noise. Principal Rodgers planted herself on the stairs to the stage, which quieted things down a little bit.

"But she didn't really have a boyfriend."

More laughter. Loud, obnoxious laughter.

"This can't be happening." My heart was pounding in my ears so loudly that I thought I might have a heart attack and die right there in the auditorium.

"It's not. It's a generic story. Probably from one of those Chicken Soup books," Tess said. But she had a death grip on my hand.

The speaker continued, even though I was praying for her to collapse or just disappear altogether. "While I love to hear of students choosing to wait, this particular story made me sad. Because this girl was making a strong and courageous choice. A choice that would protect her heart and her body in many ways. This girl wouldn't have to suffer through soul-ripping breakups or diseases that could affect her for years. She made a smart choice. A brave choice. But she was afraid to admit it."

I stared straight ahead, trying not to draw any attention to myself. I felt completely naked, like if I so much as breathed, everyone was going to notice and point me out.

Tess laughed and jabbed me with her elbow. "Isn't that hilarious?" She whispered, but it was a very loud whisper.

I stared at her.

She laughed again and then whispered fiercely in my ear, "Laugh."

I forced a smile onto my face. She was right. Everyone else was smiling and laughing about this lying virgin cheerleader, so I had to join the crowd. Or else I was going to look like I was the lying virgin cheerleader.

The speaker seemed unfazed by the volume of the audience. She barreled forward. "You should know that staying a virgin is the absolute smartest choice you can make for yourself."

I sat there with a dumb smile plastered on my face, trying to ignore everyone around me.

That's when I saw Liam. He was sitting in the front row with Lexi and several other kids I vaguely recognized.

Liam.

Liam knew my story.

Liam was helping out with one of the assemblies.

My nausea grew worse. I pulled Tess close and whispered in her ear, "It must have been Liam."

She pulled away and shook her head. "No way. He wouldn't."

Oh, but I had a really strong feeling that he did. And I was going to kill him.

CHAPTER 13

When the torture was finally over, I headed to the front of the auditorium—toward Liam. I had to play it cool. I had to act like everything was fine. As I walked against the stream of students, I overheard snatches of conversation.

"That was nuts, man."

"Who do you think it is?"

"It's so obvious."

I kept moving, honing in on my target. Liam was standing near the stage, as if he was waiting to talk to the evil speaker. He saw me and came over.

"Hey. I looked for you but—"

I cut him off. "Can we talk? Privately."

"Sure." He looked toward the speaker and then back at me. "You okay?"

I headed for the side exit of the auditorium, which led to the music and drama departments. I didn't even turn around to see if he was following. There were kids heading to classes. No privacy. I tried the door to a custodian closet, and it opened. Miracle of miracles.

Liam followed me in, his eyebrows knit together in confusion.

I closed the door and spun around to face him.

"How could you?" My voice cracked. I had meant to ask him before accusing him, but I was unable to hold back. "You told her; you had to have told her."

"Mallory. It's okay. You shouldn't be ashamed of it."

"Well, I am. And it wasn't your story to tell. That's my choice!"

"I'm sorry. I didn't think . . ."

"No, you didn't. I share my most private secret with you, and you tell the entire school? In an assembly?" The tears started then, and he reached for me. I knocked his hands off my shoulders. "Don't touch me!"

"Mallory, please."

I tried to push past him, but he jammed his foot against the base of the door.

"Let me explain. Please?"

I kept my back to him. Just because I was trapped didn't mean I had to listen to him.

"Mrs. Whittaker came the other day. I told her about you because I really think it's amazing and sad that you felt like you had to lie. I didn't think she'd repeat it here! And I didn't tell her your name."

I whirled around. "She said 'cheerleader,' Liam. Think about it. How long before everyone in this school knows exactly who she was talking about?"

"She didn't say it was someone from this school."

"She doesn't have to! Everyone assumed it; and since they're right, I'm screwed."

I wiped at my tears and turned away again.

"Mallory. I'm so sorry."

"Just let me go."

I heard him move. I grabbed the door handle, flung the door open, and sprinted out of the closet, then down the hallway.

I needed to get as far away from Liam Crawford as humanly possible.

But since we had the same stupid class for second period, he showed up in the room less than two minutes after I did. I refused to look in his direction. I felt my phone buzz in my bag. Mr. Petrini was writing on the board. I nonchalantly picked it up and read Tess's text message.

was it him

I wrote back **yes** before Petrini turned around. Texting during class was punishable by death, so I didn't try again, but Tess gave me a look of total sympathy.

It didn't help.

Especially since every conversation seemed to be about the mystery cheerleader. I was definitely getting scrutinizing looks from people. I knew they were thinking, *Could she be the virgin?*

There were about two dozen cheerleaders for fall sports. I mostly cheered for football, but sometimes I cheered for soccer when they were short. Several of the girls had long-distance boyfriends, and technically I didn't have one anymore. Maybe that would throw people off the trail.

I was also relieved to overhear a number of kids who thought the speaker made up the story . . . since they doubted a cheerleader would be a virgin. It didn't help the reputation of the sport much, but it was good for me.

By lunch I thought that maybe, just maybe, it might all blow over.

I sat down with Tess. Liam appeared at our table, no lunch in hand, and got on his knees next to my chair.

"Talk to me, please?"

"You're an idiot, Liam. She doesn't want to talk to you," Tess said.

"Yes, I'm an idiot. I agree. Look, I've been telling as many people as possible that the story was made up. I don't think anyone thinks it's true, anyway."

I hoped he was right, but I still had doubts. "Just go away," I said.

"Don't do this. This is good, you and me."

My chest tightened. It *was* good. But I couldn't trust him. You had to be able to trust people to have a relationship with them.

Liam didn't move, and I avoided his eyes. Tess stood up, brushed off her hands, and pulled Liam up by the arm. She walked away from the table with him, talked for a couple minutes, and then came back without him.

"What did you say to him?"

"Don't worry about it. I got rid of him."

I glanced around to see where he went but saw no sign of him. I let out a defeated sigh. "Why'd he have to turn out to be such a jerk?" I asked. "I really liked him."

"I know. Maybe that means you'll forgive him."

"He doesn't deserve it."

"People rarely do. But if we love them, we do it, anyway."

I looked at Tess, who still loved her mom even with what she did every day. But a guy was different than a mom, so maybe the rule didn't apply. Surely there were more guys out there. It didn't have to be Liam. I tried to bolster my courage. Just because Liam Crawford was amazing and adorable and wrote me a song . . .

I shook my head. Liam was my first attempt at a real relationship since killing off Todd. I could try again, couldn't I?

I stayed close to Tess as we left the cafeteria and tried to ignore the conversations around us. Teenagers bore quickly, so maybe no one would really care about it for too long. We walked into the lobby and saw Yvie and Sophie huddled by the stairs, talking. When they saw us, they turned—and scowled.

"It's you," Yvie said. No question. Her height made her seem all the more intimidating.

"Always had a million excuses, didn't you? You were lying to us that whole time." Sophie shook her head at me, making her short black hair swing across her shoulders.

Yvie crossed her arms and glared at Tess. "I guess you were in on the whole thing, too. I hate it when people make me feel stupid." She rested her glare on me. "I'm not stupid. I trusted you, Mallory."

Yvie started to walk away, and Tess grabbed her and pulled her back.

"Don't you dare defend her," Yvie said.

"I'm not. Mallory knows she messed up. But we're friends," Tess said.

"Not anymore." Yvie swung around, and they walked away.

"Don't worry. They'll get over it." Tess put her arm around my shoulder.

"But she'll tell," I said.

"Yeah. She probably will."

If ever there was a day I wanted to disappear, it was this one. I was excused from fourth period early since I had to change for the pep rally. But I just wanted to go home. The only thing keeping me there was that staying made me look innocent. At least more innocent than running home.

When I turned down the hallway where the cheerleaders and football players were gathering outside the locker rooms, I knew something had shifted. I'm not sure what tipped me off more, the searing looks from the cheerleaders or the grins on the football players' faces.

I slowed my walk. *Everything is going to be fine. No one knows for sure.*

Greg Paterson stepped out of the group.

"You doing okay?" He slipped his arm around my shoulder. I thought about knocking it off, but I didn't want to draw any unnecessary attention to myself.

"Yeah, I'm fine. Why?" I hoped that my face matched my words.

"You know, a lot of people think you're the virgin cheerleader."

Hearing a guy say it out loud, even if it was just Greg, made my stomach turn. There was no escaping the reality of my life.

"Who, me?" I forced out a laugh. "That's a good one."

"Then go out with me after the game tonight," he said.

Liam's face drifted into my thoughts. We were over. Weren't we? Greg was kind of a player and had dated at least a third of the squad. But I also couldn't deny that saying yes to Greg might make this whole thing go away faster.

"Sure. That'd be great. I've gotta change now."

He let me go, and I put my head down as I passed by some of the girls near the locker room door.

I looked for Tess and found her in front of the mirrors, primping.

As soon as she saw me, she grabbed me and hauled me into one of the showers, yanking the curtain closed.

"It's all over. Everyone thinks it's you."

"I'm gonna be sick."

"No, you're not. You're going to remember that you're brave, and you're gonna go out there and face them." Tess shook my shoulders. "Mallory. We'll laugh about this one day. Trust me. No fear."

She shoved me out of the shower with orders to go change. No one said anything while I changed or while I worked on getting my hair up and tying my ribbons. Everyone just stared or glared until it was time for our meeting.

We gathered at the far end of the locker room. Tara stood up with her clipboard in hand but looked right at me. "So, Mallory, is it true?" she asked point-blank. As the captain, she probably only cared about the reputation of the squad, but it felt as if everyone was holding her breath, waiting to see what I'd say.

"Is what true?" I mustered as much wide-eyed confusion as possible.

"It's a ridiculous rumor. You should know a thing or two about those, Tara," Tess said.

"I expected you to defend her, Tess. But I want to hear it from her."

All eyes shifted back to me, and I froze. *Lie and deny. Or come clean.* Those were my only two choices. My instinct was to lie and deny. After all, there was no proof. But this wasn't a court; this was high school. They could prosecute, convict, and execute me with no evidence whatsoever.

I had promised to stop lying. But when I worked on Step 8—making a list of those I had wronged—I hadn't thought about the people in front of me. But I *did* lie to them. Over and over. Clearly, it was time to start Step 9 and make amends. I was wrong to lie to everyone. To pretend to be something that I wasn't. Here was my chance to confess and apologize in one fell swoop.

If I could just get my mouth to work.

"Mallory, this is serious. We have a code of conduct for every cheerleader, and if you've betrayed the trust of the squad, we may have to cut you from the team."

There was a collective gasp.

"You can't throw her off the squad," Tess said.

"I can and I will," Tara said. "Unless she tells the truth and apologizes."

Everyone was staring again, and I looked at Tess, who shrugged and urged me on with her eyes.

I closed mine, but I could still feel everyone else's eyes boring into my soul.

"Come on. We have to warm up," someone said.

"Fine," I said. I opened my eyes and pretended it was Liam in the closet again, feeling the anger course through me. "I'm a virgin. Happy?"

I ignored the laughter and the whispers around me. Tara shifted her weight and crossed her arms, waiting for more.

"I made up a long-distance boyfriend because I didn't want the boys right through that wall to be discussing what I did or didn't do with them. You all know they do. My sex life—or the fact that I didn't want to have a sex life—wasn't anybody's business but my own."

"But you still lied," Tara said.

"I know. But who in this room hasn't lied at some point? A fake boyfriend can't pressure you like a real one. He can't go running back telling stories to his friends about what you did. And he can't convince you to do something you don't want to do in the first place." I had everyone's attention.

"My sister slept around in college, and it wrecked her life so much that she almost killed herself."

"Darby? No way," Tara said.

"Yes, Darby. I never want to go through what she did. I lied so I wouldn't have to."

I could tell from the look on Tara's face that I had won. I wouldn't be kicked off the team. But everyone was whispering around me now. I suddenly had a horrible feeling that I shouldn't have said anything about Darby.

"Look, you guys can't say anything about Darby. That's in confidence."

Heads nodded all around me, but I wasn't stupid. That was a juicy tidbit of information.

"All right. Let's get ready, girls." Tara clapped her hands, and the group followed her.

Tess hung back and waited for me. "Darby tried to kill herself? Talk about secrets."

"I'm sorry. I've never said that out loud to anybody."

"Wow. Well, you've certainly given them something besides you to focus on."

"You don't think they'll say anything, do you?"

Tess just raised an eyebrow at me and pushed open the door to the gym.

Coming clean might have a much bigger cost than I realized.

CHAPTER 14

I had to force myself to be peppy and to dance and smile at the rally. Looking out into the stands, I noticed death stares and even a couple of rude hand gestures. I tried to ignore them and just cheer.

Liam sat in the front row and never took his eyes off me. And even though it was a little mean, I purposely draped my arm over Greg's shoulder and let him pick me up to wave into the crowd.

It worked. Liam looked upset after that. I tried to console myself with the fact that it was his own fault and that I didn't have any reason to feel guilty. But I did.

After the rally I spotted Lexi as we were filing back into the locker room. She came over and asked if she could talk to me.

"I'm sorry," she said when we were alone. "I misjudged you."

"Okay." I wasn't sure how to respond.

"I was surprised to find out that lady was talking about you. I guess I never thought about what it's like for you. How the pressure would be totally different. I get it. I get why you lied about it."

She glanced away; and when I followed her gaze, I saw Liam sitting in the hallway. "Liam really likes you," she said, her voice wistful.

I liked him, too. I looked back at Lexi, her eyes wet with

tears, and I realized that maybe Liam would be better off with someone like her. *She* probably wouldn't make a date with a football player just to prove a point. They fit together better. And I knew it.

"It's okay, Lexi. I forgive you."

"Thanks." She gave me a sad smile and walked away toward Liam.

Liam caught my eye long enough for me to see that I had hurt him, again. My regret was starting to outweigh my anger. But I couldn't make myself go over to him.

Instead, I went back into the locker room to get my stuff and sat down on the bench, exhausted. Tricia, one of the few sophomores on the squad, started pulling her bags out of her locker. She glanced over, then sat down next to me.

"I'm a virgin, too," she whispered, barely loud enough for me to hear.

She scooted even closer. "I'm glad I'm not the only one," she said in my ear. She hugged me and then jumped back up with a grin on her face.

Tess came around the corner. "You ready to go?"

I nodded, grabbed my bag, and followed her out.

Tess picked me up later to head to the game, which was at another high school. It was always harder to cheer at away games because the crowds were smaller. But this was a rival team, so I hoped more people would come. I wondered if Liam would be there.

I didn't want it to be true that Liam would be better off with Lexi or someone like her. I just wanted to forgive him. I didn't feel so angry anymore.

And Tess was tense and distracted, which made me wonder if things were crazy at her house.

"How's your mom?" I asked.

"Her hand's getting better. She hates it when I change the bandage, though."

"That's not what I meant."

"The same."

"Darren?"

"He hasn't shown up, so that's good news."

My phone buzzed. A sudden hope ran through me that maybe it was Liam. But it was just my mom wanting to know where I would be.

I spoke with her, then hung up. "Oh, no. I just remembered I have a date tonight."

"You made up with Liam? When did that happen?"

"It's with Greg."

"Greg Paterson? Are you serious?"

"He asked, I was mad, I said yes." I rubbed my face with my hands. "What am I gonna do?"

"That was pretty stupid."

"Thanks."

"Just break it. Tell him you have other plans."

"I guess. But what if things don't work out with Liam?"

"You can do better than Greg. He's got more muscles than brains. Trust me."

After we got to the field and set up everything, I sat on the bench, trying to decide what to do. I figured that if there was any chance Darby was right and God did care about the small things, it couldn't hurt to try.

So I prayed. Kind of. I mean, I still wasn't sure what it was supposed to sound like, but I knew I needed help. And right afterward I got this funny feeling that I shouldn't go out with Greg, no matter what happened with Liam.

Whether the funny feeling was me or God, I wasn't sure. But I felt good about it. That is, until I spotted Liam walking up the bleachers. With Lexi.

I bumped Tess's arm. "He's with Lexi."

"Just because he's with her doesn't mean he's *with* her."

Despite getting rid of my Todd delusion, I was still obviously delusional. I couldn't even trust my own thoughts anymore. An hour ago I was sure they should be together and then I see them together and want to rip them apart. *What's wrong with me?*

And at that moment Greg walked up to the bench and wrapped his arms around me. "Hey, baby, we still on for tonight?" He stuck his face into my neck, and I squirmed out of his arms.

"Watch it," I warned him.

Greg held up his hands. "Later, then." He trotted off.

"I told you," Tess said.

"I'll tell him."

And I meant to, but through the whole game I just watched Lexi and Liam. Liam barely looked at me, so why did he drive all the way to the game? I was mad. So mad that when the game ended and Greg was waiting outside the locker room, I waved at Tess and said, "I'll call you later!"

She looked stunned, and it gave me some measure of satisfaction. After all, it wasn't very often that Tess was stunned.

Greg never stopped talking. By the time he pulled up to Sonic (not exactly a date place, if you ask me), he had recounted every successful pass he'd made during the game.

I was so bored, but too hungry to complain much. He ordered two meals and then asked me what I wanted. I asked for a wrap. He ordered it, then turned back to me. I really thought he was going to change the subject, but he hadn't talked about the second half yet.

Once we got the food, he pulled out of the parking lot and parked farther down the road, where they were building a new strip mall. It was dark, but there were streetlights nearby. Greg polished off two burgers, an order of fries and Tator Tots, and chugged down thirty-two ounces of Coke before he ever came up for air. *Gross.*

"So where do you want to go?" he asked. He wiped his mouth with the back of his hand and shoved the last of his trash into a bag.

"Home," I said.

"It's early. Come on. Let's go somewhere private."

And even naive, fake-boyfriend me could tell exactly what he was talking about. He slipped his hand onto my thigh.

I picked it up and removed it.

He snickered. "So you really are the virgin, huh?"

"What does that matter?"

He moved his hand back, but I blocked him. "It doesn't. I think it's kind of sexy."

"Really? Well, then you should find this super sexy." I picked up my drink and, in one quick motion, yanked the top off and poured the whole thing into his lap.

Before he could react, I jumped out and slammed the door.

He jammed the car into gear and squealed his tires, kicking up gravel and dust all around me.

That went well.

I pulled my cell phone out of my purse as I headed back toward Sonic. Tess didn't pick up, but I didn't want to call home. I tried twice more, then got her on the third try.

"What?" she demanded.

"I'm sorry, Tess, but I need a ride."

"I told you Greg was a bad idea."

"You were right. You told me so. Fine. Just come pick me up, please?"

Tess grew quiet, so quiet that I thought I lost the call. "Tess?"

"I can't leave right now," she whispered.

"Tess! I'm stranded."

"I. Can't."

"What's going on?" I stopped underneath a streetlamp close to the Sonic, relieved to be near people again. I felt conspicuous but safe.

"Darren."

"Take Ashley and get out of the house."

"If only it were that simple."

I heard yelling in the background and then Tess's voice. "I've got to go." The line went dead.

I looked around. I was miles from home. I looked for anybody familiar, but there was no one.

I tried my house but didn't bother leaving a message. I even tried both of my parents' cell numbers, and they didn't pick up. It dawned on me a few minutes later that Mom had said they were going to the movies. Of course their phones would be off. But it was really strange for them to leave Darby. Maybe she was home, studying.

I tried Darby's number. She picked up on the second ring.

"Mallory?"

"Hey, Darby."

"Are you okay?"

"Yeah, I'm fine, but I kind of need a ride home."

"I'm kind of on a date."

"A date? Seriously?"

"Yes, seriously. Why are you so surprised?"

Um, maybe because Mom hadn't mentioned it. Actually, we had all wondered if she'd ever date again. I didn't point out that she hadn't dated anyone since coming home from college. A date was major progress. I couldn't ruin it for her. Besides, my mom would kill me.

"Never mind, I'll figure it out." I could hear a hushed conversation and then Darby came back on.

"We'll come get you. Tell me where you are."

I tried to protest, but since I was desperate, I didn't try too hard. After saying good-bye, I sat on the curb to wait.

I was still worried about Tess. I couldn't call her back since she probably wouldn't answer, anyway. I wanted to go over there, make sure she was okay. She'd be mad, but what else could I do?

I paced, trying to make up my mind while I waited; but by the time a silver sedan pulled up, I was no closer to deciding what to do.

Darby's window came down, and there in the driver's seat was Brian. *Darby is on a date with Liam's brother?*

"Hop in," she said, a smile on her face.

I got in the back.

"Nice to see you again, Mallory. Under better circumstances," Brian said. He pulled out and started driving toward my house.

"Yeah. Thanks for your help. And the ride."

"What happened?" Darby asked.

"It's no big deal." I felt like an intruder. "I'm sorry for interrupting your night."

"It's no problem," they both said at the same time. This made them laugh and smile at each other. I slumped in the back.

"Liam didn't do anything, did he?" Brian asked.

"No."

"Good, because I can talk some sense into him for you if you'd like."

"It's not Liam."

Darby turned around in her seat. "You sure you're okay?"

I nodded. Reassuring her was nearly second nature.

Back home, I decided I had to go check on Tess. I so needed a car. I threw my bag on the porch, tucked my cell into my pocket, and started walking.

It was a really nice night, and it felt good to stretch my legs after cheering. I ran through the whole day in my head, trying to figure out if I could salvage anything at all.

Tess's house came into view, but it looked dark. Her Jeep was in the driveway, though, along with her mom's hatchback. I walked onto the porch. There were lights on in the house, but the curtains were pulled tight. I couldn't see anything. I pressed my ear to the door and listened.

Nothing.

I opened the gate and went around back. They were

definitely home. Tess's and Ashley's rooms were both dark, but the kitchen area was bright. I hunched down, moved up onto the deck, and hid under the kitchen window. Now I could hear voices. Well, really only one voice. And since it was male, it had to be Darren's.

I stood up next to the window and peered in. I could see Darren pacing and hear him yelling. Mrs. Howard was wringing her hands and stumbling around after him, crying. Every time she reached for him, he pushed her off.

Then I saw Tess. She was sitting at the kitchen table next to the wall. The table made a barrier between them. She was watching, her hands folded and pressed against her mouth. I wanted to signal her, but I couldn't without alerting Darren.

Suddenly Darren turned, and I ducked down. The voices were muffled; but I could hear a lot of cursing, and Mrs. Howard kept yelling, "Please, baby, please."

I didn't understand how she could call that nasty man "baby." She was smart and was even successful before she started drinking. But she always had lousy taste in men.

I didn't like eavesdropping, and since Tess seemed okay, I decided to go. I stood slowly to see if I could get another glimpse of what was happening before I left.

Darren was standing with his arms out, screaming at Mrs. Howard, who was now out of sight, likely on the floor.

And in his right hand was a gun.

CHAPTER 15

Darren waved the gun around in the air and yelled toward the floor, where I figured Mrs. Howard was. I moved so I could see Tess, who was still sitting quietly. If she was afraid, I couldn't tell.

I sank back down on the deck, my mind racing.

I looked at my phone and started dialing even before I sneaked off the porch. I moved into the shadows near the fence.

"Nine-one-one, what's your emergency?"

All of a sudden, what sounded like a dozen dogs started barking, the noise coming from every direction. Then floodlights lit up the backyard, and I heard the sliding glass door of Tess's house open.

"Who's out there?" Darren yelled.

I moved into the one corner where there was no light. A huge mistake. The gate to the fence was on the other side of the yard, and I wasn't going to be able to scale the fence.

"Nine-one-one, what's your emergency?"

Darren was out on the porch now, peering around the yard. I couldn't speak, or even breathe.

"Where are ya? I know you're out there. You left the stupid gate open. Trying to rob me, huh?" Darren stumbled down the stairs into the grass, walking and pointing the gun around. "Scared, huh? Shut up!" he yelled. The dogs were still barking.

Darren started toward the corner I was in. He moved slowly, peering as if he was trying to adjust to the light, and then he pointed the gun at me.

"Gotcha."

"9045 Conrad Street. Hurry." I said the words as Darren lunged at me. He snatched the phone out of my hand and tossed it over the fence. He grabbed my shoulder and a chunk of my hair, then dragged me up the deck stairs and threw me into the bright light of the kitchen. I tripped forward and fell to the floor.

"Mallory!" Tess said.

"You sit down." Darren pointed the gun at her.

I stood up and backed away. Darren was laughing, and then, just like that, he sneered and pointed the gun at me. "You call the cops?" he asked.

I stole a glance at Tess. She held one of her hands flat and moved it toward the floor. *Calm down,* she was telling me. I felt as if every muscle was trembling. I could barely stand.

Darren stepped closer; the smell of booze and cigarettes was nauseating. Mrs. Howard was whimpering on the floor. Darren pressed the gun to my chin. Until that moment the whole thing had seemed surreal. As if it were someone else's story. But the gun felt hard and very real. It occurred to me that I could actually die right here and now. My whole body tensed.

"Who. Did. You. Call?" Darren's breath came out in puffs of noxious air.

"You better take off, Darren. The cops'll be here any minute," Tess said calmly.

"You put her up to this?" Darren whipped the gun toward her.

She didn't even flinch.

Darren looked at Tess, then back at me, and then shoved his revolver in the front of his filthy jeans.

"Don't think this is over." At that moment we all heard the faint whir of sirens.

Darren spat on the floor but took off out the back door as the sirens grew louder and louder.

"Leave," Tess said. She started moving around the room, righting chairs and cleaning things up.

I followed her into the living room. "Tess?"

"What are you doing here? I had it under control." Tess didn't even stop to look at me. She grabbed some glass liquor bottles as the sirens came closer.

"Under control? He was waving a gun around." I searched Tess's face for some clue as to how we both could see the same thing and yet still see something completely different.

"I know how to handle him. You should have stayed out of it." Her voice got harder, angrier, as she kept talking. "Now I have to deal with the cops and explain—Mallory, get out of here!" This time it was an order.

"I was trying to help."

Blue and red lights flashed over us as at least two patrol cars pulled up out front.

"Go out the back. Wait until they're inside and then go home. *Now.*"

Someone pounded on the door. "Police. Open up!"

Tess pointed to the back; and I turned and left, feeling hurt, confused, and angry. She didn't seem like the same Tess I had always known. This Tess was someone I had never met, and was kind of sorry I had.

I closed the sliding door and hurried around to the gate.

She told me to wait, but I just wanted to go home. The side yard was dark, but I kept running, straight into something solid.

"Whoa there, slow down. Where are you off to?" The man's voice was calm, and he had me by the shoulders. He flipped on a flashlight, and I could see the uniform. He let me go, then flicked the flashlight toward the house.

"Were you in there?"

I nodded. I should have just smiled and shrugged my shoulders. But no, I picked this moment to tell the truth.

"Are you the one who called?"

I nodded again.

He smiled at me and wasn't the least bit threatening. After Darren, he was a welcome sight. "Let's go back inside so we can talk about what happened."

I shook my head. "I can't."

"Why not?"

"I have to get home."

He nodded. "I understand. I'll drive you."

"It's only a few blocks. I walk it all the time."

"Now see, here's the problem. I can't let you go off by yourself. And besides, we still need to talk. Come on."

He turned but stayed right beside me. *I could run. One quick duck and I'd be down the road.* But then what would happen? Would I be the one in trouble?

So I followed him to his car and crawled in the back when he opened the door. He talked to another officer for a couple of minutes and then climbed into the driver's seat.

At least he left off the lights and sirens. I told him where to go, hoping that everyone was still out. But my parents' SUV was in the driveway, and the porch lights were on. It occurred to me that I was the only one who really knew anything. So I didn't need to admit to what I'd seen. I quickly pulled my story together: I was outside and heard yelling, got scared, and called 9-1-1. But it turned out to be nothing.

Simple.

The officer opened the door for me.

"Thanks for the ride," I said.

He followed me up to the porch. Just as I was about to open the door, he stopped me and rang the doorbell.

My dad answered, and a look of panic crossed his face. "Are you okay? Is Darby okay? What's wrong?"

"Sir. I'm Officer Vasser. Everything's just fine."

"Ryan? Who is it?" My mom appeared in the doorway and went through the same questions as my dad, only more frantically.

"If I could come inside, I'll explain everything," Officer Vasser said.

On the way to the living room, my mom switched gears. "Did you do something? What did you do?"

I slumped into a chair while my parents hovered on the edge of the couch. Officer Vasser explained what had happened and why he'd brought me home.

"I just needed to hear your daughter's version of the events. For the report, you know."

"Of course, of course." My dad gestured toward me. "Ask her anything you'd like."

Officer Vasser and my parents all turned to stare at me.

And I told them my story. It was actually true—just minus a few details. I feigned ignorance at his other questions. When the officer was satisfied, my parents showed him to the door and then returned to the living room.

My mom planted her hands on her hips. "Is that what really happened?"

"Yes."

"What aren't you telling us?" Dad asked.

"Nothing."

Dad sat on the coffee table in front of me. He looked older, grayer. When had that happened? "Mally, listen. We know something's going on at Tess's, but this is serious. We've stayed out of it up till now; but when the police are being called, well, we can't stay out of it anymore."

"Can we do this tomorrow?" I asked. "Please."

Mom and Dad exchanged a look and then nodded. I stood up, feeling exhausted. I just wanted to close my eyes and not think.

They enveloped me in a hug. I didn't pull away. I felt too safe. But when I finally did, I saw tears in the corners of my mom's eyes.

"You can tell us anything—you know that, right?"

I nodded. But it wasn't my story to tell.

I woke up on Saturday with a pounding headache, so I stayed in bed, listening to the rain drumming on the roof. Perfect weather for my mood.

Tess.

I dreaded finding out what had happened with the police, her mom. My parents were way past suspicious. They didn't even know yet about me calling Darby for help. I wasn't sure if they knew Darby was on a date, but if they found out I had interrupted something so important . . . I couldn't think about it.

My room seemed so bare without Todd. That fantasy world was so much simpler than the real one I was now dealing with. I could impose rules and structure on a fictional life, but my real life had dissolved into chaos, and I didn't know what to do about it.

Someone knocked on my door softly, then cracked it open.

"You up?" my mom asked.

I turned over to face her. She came in with one of her three dozen teacher mugs in her hand. She was wearing yoga pants, and her hair was still messy with sleep. She sat on the edge of my bed and put her arm on my leg.

I thought back to Tess's mom whimpering on the floor. *I'm a lucky girl.*

"I know balancing confidences can be hard. And sometimes people ask us to keep secrets for good reasons. And sometimes they ask us to for bad reasons. I promise you, Mallory, if you tell me what's going on, I'm not going to do anything on my own. I just want to help you figure it out. Whatever it is."

"You'll want to tell. You won't be able to help yourself." I pulled myself into a sitting position and leaned back on the headboard. "I know you."

"I'm not saying I won't want to. But I'm really worried. And I need to know what's going on. We can't keep secrets from each other. I don't want you to . . . to ever feel like . . . like Darby did." Mom's voice cracked, and she pressed her fist to her mouth.

"Mom, I'm not suicidal."

"I didn't think Darby was either."

And that was it in a nutshell.

I had to tell my mom something. But what could I say that wouldn't worry her more? The gun thing was out, but maybe the rest. I decided to start off slow.

"Tess's mom drinks."

Mom nodded. "Okay, how much?"

"A lot."

Slowly, the main parts of the story spilled out: the drinking, Tess's worries about foster care, Darren's behavior (minus the detail about the gun). I was sure that would send my mom right over the edge. She nodded a lot and urged me to continue, all the while sipping her coffee.

When I was done, Mom didn't say anything for several minutes.

"You want to tell, don't you?"

"Absolutely. Don't you?"

"Well, yeah. But what will happen to Tess if I do?"

"What will happen to Tess if you don't?"

Good point.

My mom shook her head. "It may be out of your hands, anyway. If the police were there last night and saw her mom's condition, well, they may have already called social services to investigate."

"No!"

"I mean, it would be up to them, based on what they saw, but it's within their power to do it. Especially if she was drunk."

Now I was scared. If something did happen, it would be my fault for calling the police. Tess would blame me, and she would have every right to.

"Let's go to the mall in a little while, grab some lunch.

Do something completely normal. What do you say?" she asked.

"Sure."

Mom left, and I went to take a very long shower. I wanted to call Tess, but since she hadn't called me, I assumed the worst. And I really didn't want to know if I was right.

It wasn't until I was getting dressed that I realized my phone was in someone's backyard, currently getting drenched, if a dog hadn't already eaten it. Tess could have been calling me for hours and I wouldn't know it.

When I came downstairs, Darby was talking with my mom at the kitchen table.

"You didn't tell me Darby had to pick you up last night," Mom said, her voice even but laced with frustration.

"Mom, I told you, I didn't mind. I'm glad she called." Darby smiled at me.

"How was the rest of your date?" I asked.

"Wonderful."

And I could tell from the look on her face that she was really happy, happier than I had seen her in a long time.

"Brian seems awfully serious," I commented. I didn't say how worried I was that maybe she couldn't handle it. What would she do if Brian flaked out like Liam did?

"Oh, but he's not! He's funny and so smart, and he loves God. It's a trifecta. And we're going out again tonight."

I wondered if the same thoughts that went through my head had gone through my mom's as well. She looked happy for Darby, but there was worry there, too.

Finding a guy was one thing. Finding a guy who could deal with Darby's past and the fact that she might not be able to have children was something else. They were just beginning to date, though, so it was probably too early. But still . . . it hovered in the air around us, spoiling some of the joy.

At least for Mom and me. Darby was positively giddy.

"Hey, can I come to the mall with you guys?" she asked. "I want to get something new for tonight."

The more the merrier.

CHAPTER 16

In the end, I bowed out of going to the mall. I needed to know what happened with Tess. And I wasn't sure I wanted to hear about how wonderful Brian was all morning.

Mom barely acknowledged me when I said I was staying home. I think she was too happy about Darby's mood to mind.

Once they left, I pulled on a waterproof jacket with a hood and set out for Tess's. The weather was dreary, and I felt the same way inside.

I was happy for Darby, really. But since Brian was linked to Liam, it made me think about him and the assembly and how I thought he was the perfect guy, too—until he stabbed me in the back.

Tess's house was completely quiet again. I decided to see if I could find my cell phone. Even if the phone itself was ruined, maybe the chip inside would be okay. I knocked on the neighbor's door. An older couple lived there, but I didn't really know them.

A gray-haired man wearing khaki pants and a baggy cardigan answered the door, a cup of coffee in his hand.

"Hi. I'm sorry to bother you." I quickly explained that my phone was in their backyard. "Would you mind if I look for it?"

The man opened the door wider. "Feel free. But there's probably not much hope for it, is there?"

"Maybe not, but it can't hurt to try."

I stepped inside and followed him through the house to the back. A small terrier came running out of the kitchen, barking at my feet.

"Hush, Tiger. Leave the poor girl alone." An older woman wearing a purple running suit and lots of fancy jewelry appeared in the doorway. "You're drenched to the bone, child!"

The man filled her in on my cell phone.

"You sure you even want to bother with it?" she asked.

"Yes, if you don't mind."

The man slid open the door, and I ran right, toward Tess's house, figuring Darren didn't toss it too far. It wasn't hard to find: a bright-red spot on the soggy green grass. I snatched it up and ran back inside the house.

I stood on the towel that someone had placed just inside the door.

"What are you doing here?" It was Tess.

I pulled my hood back.

"Tess? What are *you* doing here? Are you okay? What happened?" I didn't want to move until I stopped dripping all over the place.

Tess just stood there, her eyes slicing through me. The couple had moved out of sight somewhere, taking the little dog with them.

"Tess. Please try to understand. I got scared when I saw that gun. And when he was coming toward me . . . I panicked."

Tess crossed her arms. "I understand perfectly. And I need you to understand that you've ruined absolutely everything. So take your phone and go home."

"What happened?" I took a step toward her, but her glare stopped me.

"What do you think? The police took my mom to the hospital and called social services. Happy?"

"No."

"It's what you wanted, isn't it? All along you've been wanting me to tell, and instead of helping me, you just go and do what you want, anyway. Some friend." She turned and left the room.

I walked toward the front door.

The woman came down the stairs and stopped me. She rubbed my shoulder. "Tess is upset, but she'll come around."

"I doubt it. She's right. It's my fault." I couldn't stop the tears.

"Now look here." The woman, who was a head shorter than me, grabbed my shoulders and pulled me close. "That girl needed help. You knew it, and I knew it. But you did something about it. Not everyone has the gumption to do what's right, even if it makes other people mad. Mark my words. She'll thank you for it someday." She pulled me into a hug. "You hang in there. It'll all work out."

I thanked her and walked home. If only that woman was right.

I set myself up on the couch with a bunch of movies and plenty of Doritos and Dr Pepper: my version of a pity party. Since I couldn't actually disappear, it was the best I could do.

I was watching *The Proposal* when my dad came in and set down his four camera bags.

I waved.

"You by yourself?" he asked. "Where did Mom go?"

"She's at the mall with Darby."

Dad stepped into the mudroom to take off his shoes and coat, then came over and sat on the couch with me.

"I thought you were working all day," I said.

"The rain. I had about six teams lined up for shots today, and then it goes and rains. I hate rescheduling everything."

"I'll help if you want me to," I said.

"Thanks. I may just take you up on that." He stood and stretched. "Oh, and I talked to the Garrisons last week. They have that photo collage you made hanging over their fireplace in a huge thirty-by-forty frame."

I smiled.

"You feeling all right?"

"Yeah. I'm tired."

"Okay. I think I'm going to go finish up the Briggses' wedding pictures." He opened the door to the basement, where he had his full office and workroom set up, and went downstairs.

I settled back in with my movie, but less than ten minutes later, the garage door flew open, and Darby came running through the house and up the stairs. Then Mom walked inside, avoiding my eyes. Her face was red and splotchy.

"What's wrong?" I was almost scared to ask.

Mom finally looked at me, but it wasn't a warm, loving look. No, this look was accusing and angry. Kind of the same look Tess had used on me.

"Who did you tell?"

I sat up, scared. "Tell?"

"About her getting sick, her attempt, everything?"

The air seemed to leave the room as I tried to grab at the thoughts swirling around in my head.

"What do you mean?" I asked, hoping beyond hope that it had nothing to do with me.

Mom seemed to lose all patience. She was never much of a yeller, but her voice grew higher with each word. "Somehow, people know about Darby getting sick. How would they possibly know unless someone said something? I didn't tell anyone. Darby certainly didn't tell anyone. That leaves you."

"Me?" I said. But all could think was, *The cheerleaders . . .*

Mom moved closer to the couch. "What did you do, Mallory?"

"I just, I mean, I didn't think that anyone . . ."

"That anyone would what? That it wouldn't spread around? You had no right to tell *anyone* about Darby. And now she's terrified that Brian's going to find out before she has a chance to tell him the truth. You've put her in a terrible situation. How could you do that?"

I covered my face and sobbed. When I finally moved my hands, Mom was gone and I was alone.

I hid in my room for the rest of the weekend, sneaking down only to grab some food. I had no one to talk to. No one to try and figure it out with. And each minute that passed was another minute closer to school. If the rumors about Darby had spread this much, then it was a given that by Monday morning everyone would also know that I was the virgin cheerleader. It just made my existence that much more miserable.

Of everyone, Liam was the only person who would be willing to speak to me. But I couldn't bring myself to call him. Because honestly, if he hadn't done what he did, the rest of it wouldn't have happened.

Impulsively, I pulled out the Todd box and sat on my bed with it. I didn't break the tape; I just stared at it.

If only I had kept Todd, everything would be different.

By Sunday evening I felt like the black sheep of the family. It was like Mom couldn't stand the sight of me, and Darby barely emerged from her room. Dad was the only one who tried to coax me out, and even he seemed reluctant. Dad was a peaceful kind of guy, and any fighting or tension bothered him.

Not that there was anything to argue about. I screwed up. That much was obvious.

Monday morning was bright and sunny, and I had every intention of staying in bed. But Mom came in, pulled up my shades, and stood there as I tried to adjust to the light.

"You're going to school," she said.

"I can't."

"Yes, you can. Every decision we make has a consequence, and you need to face yours. I'm leaving in thirty minutes. I want you downstairs, dressed and ready to go."

Mom left, and I wanted to cry all over again.

But I got up. I would have to deal with school sooner or later, and I might as well do it on a day I had a ride.

On my way downstairs, I stopped outside of Darby's

closed door. I wanted to apologize to her so badly, but that would mean facing her, looking her in the eye. And admitting the hurt and pain I'd caused.

Dad gave me a big hug when I got downstairs, but he ate his breakfast in silence, reading his *ShutterPro* magazine.

Mom bustled around, cleaning the kitchen and gathering papers until she looked at her watch and said, "Let's go."

I followed her obediently and sat next to her in the car.

"I messed up. I'm sorry," I said.

"I don't want to talk about this right now." She wouldn't even look at me.

I turned away and watched the houses and trees fly by, trying to come up with a strategy for school. Pretend not to be bothered by it? I could do that. I had practice with pretending.

But as much as I didn't want to think about that horrible assembly, something that woman said kept ringing in my ears. *She made a smart choice. A brave choice.* Was I smart and brave? I wanted to be. I wanted to be a girl who made choices with confidence.

I had gotten rid of Todd because I didn't want to pretend anymore, but now I wasn't sure who I really was. Could I choose to be smart and brave now, even if I wasn't before?

Mom pulled up in the circle, and I climbed out. She didn't say good-bye. It hurt, but I'd have to deal with my family later. Right now, I had to deal with North County High.

There was no Liam waiting for me. I ignored the very definite whispers as I walked to my locker.

Then I got a look at it.

Someone had written *virgin* across the red paint in thick, black marker.

I stared at it, hearing the laughter behind me and feeling the eyes waiting to see what I'd do.

My instinct was to run.

But there was nowhere to go.

I looked at the word, at its hard black lines. The word that was never meant to be a slur. And yet it was. An accusation.

You're a virgin.

Something is wrong with you.

No one wants you.

There were a few other words that would be a more accurate reflection of me. *Liar. Traitor. Hypocrite.* Pick one, any one. But I was a virgin, too. It was as true a word as any of the others. Could I accept that one as well?

I set down my backpack and searched through it until I came up with a Sharpie. I stood up and looked around at the clusters of kids watching. I turned back to the word and underlined it twice. Then I added an exclamation point, capped the pen, and opened the locker.

At least it was true.

By second period I had gotten three offers to help me lose my virginity and a lot of angry stares. I just ignored them and tried to focus on the faces in the hallways that didn't seem so angry. There were some sympathetic looks out there.

But second period meant facing Tess and Liam in the same class. I went to class early, since the hallways were the most dangerous place for overhearing things you didn't want to listen to. I looked up when I caught sight of Tess's curls. She walked to her desk and sat down, not even glancing at me.

Liam came in right behind her. He sat in his usual seat, in front of me.

"Something going on with Tess?"

"Seriously. You're going to ask about Tess? Do you hear what everyone's saying? About me? Because of you?"

"Yes. And I'm sorry. A hundred times over. You have no idea how sorry."

"Not good enough."

"Then let me show you something after class. Please?"

Mr. Petrini stood up as the bell rang. "All right. Page eighty-five."

Liam kept waiting for an answer.

"Maybe," I whispered.

He winked and turned toward the front.

CHAPTER 17

Liam stood by my desk after the bell rang. I followed him. The truth was, I wanted to forgive him. It was a monumentally stupid thing he did, but it wasn't actually his fault that I made it worse by telling Darby's secrets, too. Of course, I wasn't going to let him off easy.

He led me to his locker, which was in a different hallway than mine, and pointed at it.

"That's my locker," he said.

"So?" I started to walk away, but he reached for my arm and pulled me gently back. I looked away because those chocolate eyes were starting to melt me.

He held out a black marker to me. "Take it."

"Why?"

"I want you to write on my locker so that it matches yours. You're not the only virgin in the school, you know."

"I'm not going to write on your locker."

He shrugged. "Fine." He turned and wrote *virgin* in big letters across his locker.

"You're going to get in trouble," I said.

"I don't care. I don't want you to feel like you're all alone. Because you're not. I'm not going to leave you in this alone." He held my shoulders, and I just wanted to fall into his arms. I resisted, but barely. My resolve to stay strong was crumbling. He waited another few moments and then said, "Come on. Let's go to lunch."

So I walked with Liam to lunch, ignoring the catcalls and the comments that came our way.

I saw Tess, but she was sitting with some other cheerleaders. I got food that I probably wouldn't eat and followed Liam to a table with Lexi and a few others. I was so glad not to be alone that I didn't even care about Lexi being there.

A group of guys walked by, and one of them—a dark-haired guy I didn't know—laughed and pointed at our table. "We're in Virgin Central, guys. Who wants to start the bidding?" The whole group cracked up. He leaned in close to me and said, "Virgin cheerleaders are the tastiest."

Liam jumped to his feet and stepped in front of me, forcing the guy to back off.

The guy laughed and walked away with his group of idiots.

Lexi rolled her eyes and smiled at me sympathetically.

I pushed my food away.

Liam sat down again. "I'm so sorry this is happening."

"I know you are, it's just . . ."

"What? What can I do to make it up to you?"

"I don't know." I really didn't.

By the time practice rolled around, I was sick of trying to be smart and brave. People were just mean and cruel. But I did notice the word *virgin* on two other lockers as I went to classes. *That* was an interesting development.

It was a nice afternoon, so we went out onto the field to practice. Several of the football players, egged on by Greg, made rude gestures toward me, but I pretended it didn't bother me.

None of the cheerleaders said much, but I knew at least one of them was responsible for spreading Darby's secret outside the team. Tara kept us busy, and I didn't have time even to consider who the culprit was. Tricia, the girl who had confessed that she was a virgin, too, smiled at me the whole practice. Well, I had one fan.

During practice, I noticed Samantha Morgan sitting on a bench, taking notes and pictures. I didn't think much of it until she approached me after we were finished.

"Hey, Mallory. Do you have a minute?"

"I guess." I shoved my water bottle into my bag and zipped it up.

"I wanted to talk to you about the assembly on Friday and the lockers. On the record, though, because I want to write about it for the *The Falcon's Nest*."

The school paper.

I started walking toward the school, but she kept pace beside me. "Look, people are going to keep talking about it no matter what you do."

"I don't want to make it any worse than it already is."

Samantha stepped in front of me, effectively stopping me. "I'm going to write this story. Wouldn't you rather I have all my facts straight? Your side of the story?"

She had me there. "It's not much of a story. Why even bother?" I asked.

"It's a great story." She walked over to a bench and sat down. When I joined her, she touched a button on her phone and held it out. "Now, can you confirm that you are the cheerleader Barbara Whittiker was talking about on Friday?"

Could I? Just put it out there and be totally honest?

I supposed if I wanted to stop living a pretend life, I also needed to figure out what the real life I wanted looked like. I was pretty sure of one thing, though—a different life required different choices. Now that it was all out in the open, what was I going to do with it?

I paused, knowing that the next words out of my mouth were going to set the stage for everything else. *Strong and brave.*

"Yes. I am."

Liam was in the lobby with his guitar, playing, when I came out of the locker room. I glanced at my watch. I had talked with Samantha for more than twenty minutes, which meant he'd been waiting for a long time.

He stopped playing when he saw me. "Need a ride home?"

"Sort of."

He smiled. "Good."

He packed up his guitar, and I walked beside him out to his car. Being with him felt comfortable and safe. And with everything else that was going on, I just let it feel good.

"Have you forgiven me yet?" he asked.

"I'm still deciding."

He cocked his head. "I can live with that. For now. So what's going on with you and Tess?"

Tess. How was I going to fix things with Tess when she wouldn't even speak to me?

"It's a long story."

"I like stories."

I resisted the urge to dig at him for what happened the

last time I shared a story with him. "It's not my story to share." That was one lesson I was going to hang on to in all of this. I was only going to share my *own* stories.

"Can I do anything to help?"

"I wish you could."

Liam dropped me off at home, and I went upstairs to shower and change. I took a long one, hoping for some sort of watery inspiration about what to do. Apologizing hadn't gotten me anywhere with Tess or my mom. I still needed to try with Darby, though.

And Darby was the person I was most afraid to face. I couldn't get that image out of my head—her body lying so pale and motionless on the bathroom floor. How I thought she was already dead.

Everything was starting to get better for her, but I had to mess things up with my big mouth. I could have left her out of it. I should have. No one needed to know the real reason I didn't want to have sex.

Darby's . . . incident . . . was not a comfortable topic in my family. And my relationship with Darby had turned into nothing but a set of rules. *Don't bother her. Don't pressure her. Leave her alone.* But the last few weeks had given me these irresistible glimpses of what it might be like to have a sister again. I ached for it.

I got dressed and wandered down the hallway to Darby's room. I knew she was in there. She had barely left her room since the mall. But as I knocked and waited, I had a growing sense of dread. I hadn't seen her in hours. *What if . . . ?*

Then the door cracked open, and I was so relieved to see her that it took me a moment to notice her pale face and sad, red eyes.

"Can I come in?"

Darby looked at me for a few long seconds before she opened the door wider. I stepped inside. I loved Darby's room. She had always had a knack for decorating and had designed her room with simple white furniture and lush, colorful fabrics. She walked over to her red saucer chair and dropped into it. I perched on her bed.

"I am so sorry. Sorrier than I have ever been in my life."

"I know." The words were quiet, and she stared out the window as she spoke.

"I wish I could fix it, change it, take it back somehow . . ."

"You can't." She turned to look at me.

"Have you talked to Brian?" I regretted the question immediately, because she turned away again and began to cry, shaking her head.

"I can't face him."

"But you have to try."

She shook her head again and buried her face in her knees. "It doesn't matter, anyway."

"But it does." I went over and knelt by her chair. "Please, Darby. You can't just give up on him. You're not even giving him a chance."

Darby grew quiet again.

"I really am sorry," I said. "Some girl is writing an article about me at school, but I didn't mention your name at all. She asked, but I didn't say a thing."

"Thanks."

"Will you tell me? If I can do anything to help?"

Darby nodded, and I got up to leave.

"Mally."

"Yeah?"

"I forgive you," she said.

"Thanks." I looked at her as I closed the door—still curled up, still so sad. I was glad that she didn't hate me, but it didn't solve anything either. I wanted so badly for her to be happy.

I turned down the hallway, and my mom was standing by her door, arms crossed.

I held up my hands. "I was just apologizing."

"How is she?"

I paused. "Sad."

Mom shook her head and turned to go down the stairs. Leaving me behind.

After dinner I asked my dad if he would take me to the store so I could get a new cell phone. I had the money, but I couldn't get there on my own. He agreed, even though Mom shot him a look like he was fraternizing with the enemy.

"So why do you need a new phone?" he asked once we were in the car.

"It got wet."

He drove to the shopping center and came inside with me. My dad was a total gadget geek, so he became engrossed in all of the smartphones while I waited for one of the guys to pry my phone apart and see if he could salvage my SIM card.

I picked out a phone I could afford, but Dad showed me a cute new one with a slide-out keyboard.

"This one's got a better camera and twice the memory." He held it out for me.

"Yeah, and it's twice the cost."

He shrugged. "I'll pay the extra."

"Mom'll kill you. We're supposed to pay for all our own cell phone stuff."

He considered it. "This one is better, and if you promise not to leave it out in the rain, I'll take the heat for it."

I grinned and gave him a big hug. It was my dad's way of saying he loved me. And right then, I really needed to hear it.

We waited while the tech transferred the chip and got it all activated. When we hopped in the car, I checked my voice mail and was sad to find a bunch of nasty texts from unknown numbers. But nothing from Liam.

I closed the phone.

"Thanks, Dad. This is great."

"You're welcome. And Mom . . . she'll come around."

"I don't know. She's scary when it comes to Darby."

"It's just because she's worried."

Dad shifted in his seat, probably uncomfortable that we were speaking of the unspeakable. In its own way, though, it was a pretty big step for the two of us.

When we got home, I gave him another big hug on the front porch.

"Let's not show that to your mom just yet, okay?"

"You got it."

CHAPTER 18

Mom still wasn't talking to me on Tuesday morning, aside from absolutely necessary conversation. She dropped me off at school and left. It stung.

The lockers were hard to miss when I walked into school. Dozens of them had the word *virgin* scrawled in marker; several of them were even sporting exclamation points. I wondered if people had chosen to put it there, like Liam, or if other kids were writing it in an accusatory way. It was hard to tell.

During homeroom announcements, it became clear that the administration was *not* impressed.

"Those students who have vandalized their lockers will report to the office immediately after dismissal. Failure to report will result in an immediate ISS."

I hated being so conspicuous. I felt as if everyone was talking and whispering behind my back. On the way to PE, I had to pass Greg and his friends, who whistled and commented as I walked by. Katie came up and walked with me to the locker room.

"So which is it?"

"Huh?"

"Are you a virgin or not?"

"I am. Why?"

"Greg's saying you slept with him."

I yanked open a locker and shoved my bag inside. "Greg's a liar. He's just saying that because I *didn't* sleep with him."

Katie shrugged. "Well, you lied to everyone about Todd. . . ."

I pulled on my gym shorts and tied back my hair in a ponytail, now totally aware of what people were saying about me.

Katie leaned in. "Look, I don't care what you do; I just think you should quit acting all high and mighty about it."

"I'm not." But Katie was already gone.

I went out to the gym, where Mr. Yasbeck was lining us up to do fitness testing. Lexi stood next to me in line.

"So I guess we're in trouble," she said.

"You wrote on your locker?" I asked.

"Yeah."

"Well, I didn't write on mine. I don't know who did."

Lexi reached up to stretch her arms. "What's so bad about being labeled a virgin?"

I reached down to my toes, following Yasbeck's instructions, avoiding the question. It was fine for Lexi's sort to run around and declare their virginity to the world, but I wasn't like them. It was hard enough to admit that I was a virgin in the first place, and now people were calling me a snob for it? Great.

I got through PE and AP Euro by ignoring everything around me. It was hard not to notice that the word *slut* had started to appear on some lockers as well. And the tone of the hallways seemed angrier.

Walking to lunch was like walking through hell.

"I can take care of your little problem right now."

"Ain't no way that hasn't seen some action."

"Little Miss Snow White thinks she's all that."

The worst part was that I never asked to be a part of it. How could I escape from my own life?

Liam sat next to me at my table.

"I bet they'll make us scrub lockers. Ya think?"

I stabbed the salad with my fork.

"Mallory, it'll blow over."

I doubted that. And even if it did, it still felt as if the year had been ruined. In ten years, when I looked back on being a junior, this sequence of events would overpower everything else. I'd only remember what I'd lost.

"Come on, this is kind of funny."

"Maybe for you, Mr. Never Stays in One Place. But this is my home. These are my friends. And I've never, ever been hated. So thanks a lot for giving me my first experience as a pariah."

Liam's shoulders sagged. "You're right. I just don't know how to fix this."

I glanced over at Tess, sitting across the cafeteria. I was pretty sure I could handle everything that was happening if Tess was with me. I didn't really care if everyone else hated me, but Tess? I *needed* Tess.

Liam glumly ate his burger and picked at his fries.

When the bell rang, I ran over to intercept Tess.

"Tessie, please talk to me."

She tossed her paper tray in the garbage as we passed by the cans. She didn't even look at me.

"Did you see my locker?" she asked.

"No."

"Well, I'm sure you know which word is on it."

"I didn't want this. I didn't want any of this."

She whirled around. "Welcome to my world." Then she disappeared into the crowd.

I went straight out the lobby doors and started walking home.

I knew I would get in trouble for skipping, for not showing up at the office for whatever they wanted from us vandals. For skipping cheerleading practice. For everything. But I didn't care. I just didn't care anymore.

It took twenty minutes to walk home, but I wasn't in any hurry. I took the route to pass by Tess's house, wishing I could tell from the front yard what was going on inside the house. But it looked the same as always.

I went to my room and curled up in my bed, but I felt like I didn't even have the right to cry. Everything was my fault.

A few minutes later Darby pushed open my door.

"Oh! It's you. What are you doing home?"

That's when the tears started, and they didn't stop. At some point I realized Darby was sitting on my bed, rubbing my back. I just cried and cried and took the tissues that Darby pressed into my hand.

When there was nothing left, I rolled over onto my back and stared up at the ceiling.

"What happened?" she asked.

I looked at her, and all of my mom's instructions about Darby mingled with my own desperation to talk to someone about my mess.

Desperation won.

I spilled the story. Everything that had happened since

the assembly—was that only last week?—the lockers, the comments I even told her about Tess, about Darren and his gun pointing at my chin. The story came tumbling out so fast, I couldn't have stopped it if I wanted to.

When I finished, I looked at Darby's face for any signs of panic or trauma or depression, but she only looked concerned. "Why didn't you talk to me earlier?"

"I'm not allowed to talk to you."

Darby wrinkled her forehead. "Not allowed?"

I felt that pressure again, like I was treading too close to the truth and I should backpedal away from it.

"She . . . I mean . . . we, you know . . . just don't want you to have too much stress."

"Keep going," Darby said.

Darby kept pushing until I told her about Mom's rules and the constant reminders not to put any pressure on her.

"Wait a minute. There's actually a schedule so that I'm not home alone?" Darby looked shocked.

"Please, don't tell Mom I told you."

"That cheerleading camp this summer. Did you have to miss it . . . because of me?"

I paused, but why try to hide anything now? I nodded.

"That's why you have to work for Dad, too?"

"I like working for Dad. But, yeah, it gives me a completely flexible schedule."

Darby sat cross-legged on my bed and put her hands on her knees as if she was trying to steady herself.

"I guess we were all afraid . . . you know, that you might . . ." I couldn't say it, but Darby did.

"Try to kill myself again?"

And with those words, the words that had never been

spoken between us, I felt both a terror and a release. A terror for the fear that merely saying the words would cause them to happen. Release for the realization that by *not* saying them, I hadn't actually taken a breath in a long while.

Darby scooted even closer. "Mallory. You don't have to be scared. I'm sad right now, and I'm not sure what I'm going to do, but I'm not going to kill myself. That part of my life is over. Do you hear me?"

I did, but now that the words were out, I didn't want to stop talking about it. "That day. I thought you were already dead."

Darby grabbed me and squeezed. "I'm so sorry that you found me like that. I wasn't thinking about you, or anybody else. I was only thinking about myself. That must have been horrible for you. I can't even imagine. I'm so sorry, Mallory. What I did, that one stupid decision, it derailed us all, didn't it?"

I nodded.

"I feel like I've taken so much from you. Please forgive me." Darby wiped at her tears. And even though I had never wanted an apology from her, at that moment I saw that maybe I needed one.

"But Mallory, hear me when I say this. Even if I had died that day, it wouldn't have been your fault. You can't be responsible for someone else's decisions—the bad ones or the good ones. You don't have to protect me anymore. I'm not your job or your responsibility. I'm your big sister, and I'm supposed to be here for you. And I will be. From now on."

"Mom'll be mad at me. For talking to you," I told her.

"Mom has her own issues to work through, and those

aren't your problem either. Let's just concentrate on the things that *are* your problems."

"Okay."

"Let's start with Liam, since he's the easiest."

"Easiest? He started this whole mess."

Darby shook her head. "No, my dear, he was just the one who made it public. The mess was all yours. So cut him some slack. After all, I forgave you for going public with my secret."

Good point.

"I still can't believe you made up a boyfriend just to hide being a virgin. I mean, I'm really glad you're not sleeping around like I was, but I'm surprised you did it that way."

"Well, that was mostly because of you."

Darby looked surprised. "Me?"

"At first I just didn't want to, but then all that stuff happened with you, and I don't know, it didn't seem like having sex was worth the risk. Todd made it easier for me to avoid any pressure to do it."

Tears started slipping down Darby's cheeks, and I panicked. *Did I say too much?* I tried to think of a way to end the conversation when Darby squeezed my hand.

"Thanks for that," she said.

"For what? I didn't do anything."

"Trust me, you did. And I don't have any advice about Tess or what to do at school, but I promise I'll think about it. And I'll be praying for you." Darby reached over and hugged me, then left the room.

Strange.

Not only did I not know what to do, but my mom was going to freak when she found out that I'd confided in Darby.

Having a mom who works in the school system is a major disadvantage. Other kids could skip school and get away with it. Not me.

Mom pounded on my door at precisely 3:45. "Mallory. Are you in there? You'd better be violently ill." She pushed open the door.

"Now you're skipping school, too?"

"I'm sick," I said. Then I coughed.

"Yeah. Your principal said that you were part of some school-wide vandalism? Are you kidding me? Does this have anything to do with Darby?"

Darby? I couldn't help myself. I got mad.

"Darby? Darby? Why does everything always come back to Darby? The world doesn't revolve around Darby, Mom."

"I don't think the world . . ."

"Yes, you do. We all revolve around her like some crazy merry-go-round. It's all about making sure everything is nice and calm, that things aren't too stressful, that we stay upbeat. That we pretend that everything is perfect. Well, my life is about as messed up as I can possibly make it right now, and I can't fix any of it. I can't be upbeat or calm or nice."

Mom stared at me, surprised at my outburst, I guess.

"And just for the record, I didn't vandalize anything." I pushed past her and ran down the stairs and straight out the front door.

I automatically walked toward Tess's house, knowing she would still be at practice. There were no cars in the driveway, so I sat on her front porch.

A group of kids were playing hockey in the street, yelling

and having fun. I watched them for a while and fiddled with my new phone while I tried to figure out what I could say to Tess.

"She's not here."

I looked up to see Tess's neighbor lady standing on the driveway wearing a bright-blue running suit and lots of jewelry. She walked over and sat beside me.

"I'm Kay Baker, I don't think I formally introduced myself the other day." She held out her hand, and I shook it.

"Mallory Dane."

"I take it Tess still isn't talking to you? Well, let's see where I can fill you in. Mrs. Howard is at a rehab facility over in Orange County."

"That's good, right? I mean, she's not in jail or anything."

"Yes, that's good. If she's willing to take the help she needs. It's really up to her. Tess and Ashley are staying with Ralph and me for the time being."

"I thought they might be, but I didn't know for sure."

Kay nodded. "Ralph and I never had kids, so it's sort of like getting to be grandparents for the first time."

"So she's okay? Everything's okay then?"

Kay smiled at me and patted my hand. "Yes, it was all for the best. But Tess, she's having a hard time. She's been in charge and on her own for so long. It's a big change for her, and I'm not sure she likes it."

I could understand that.

"Mallory, you did the right thing. No matter how Tess feels about it, you did right by her. You were a true friend." Kay hugged me and stood up to leave. "Tess'll be back soon if you want to wait over at the house."

"Thanks, I'll wait here."

Kay waved and walked away.

If what I did was good, then why did I still feel so bad?

I waited around until I saw Tess's Jeep pull into her driveway. She climbed out and slammed the door, staring at me.

"What are you doing here?" Her voice was sharp.

"Waiting for you."

"Then you wasted your time." Tess threw her bag over her shoulder and walked toward the Bakers' house.

"Tess, please. Please. You've got to talk to me."

Tess whirled around. "I trusted you."

"I know."

"I asked you not to tell anyone, and you stabbed me in the back."

"I know."

"I didn't want this."

"I know. I know you didn't want help, but you *needed* it, Tess. It was too much for you, and whether you hate me forever or not, I'm glad I told. Because now your mom is getting help, and you've got someone to watch out for you. I know it's not what you wanted, but it's what you needed."

Tess's face looked angry for a second, then her shoulders relaxed a bit and her bag slipped to the ground.

"The Bakers seem really nice," I went on. "Even they knew you needed help, and they barely know you. I'm your friend, Tess. Friends fight, and they make mistakes, but real friends help each other, even when it risks everything."

Tess's scowl slipped into something sadder, but she didn't say anything. I took a few cautious steps toward her, thinking that at any minute she was going to turn and storm away. But she didn't. I got all the way over to her before she started crying.

She covered her face with her hands and sobbed, and I wrapped my arms around her. She didn't pull away.

After several minutes she began wiping her face, collecting herself.

"I'm sorry, Tess."

"Why? You just said you were glad you did it. So which is it? Are you sorry or are you glad?" A smile was playing at the corners of her lips.

"Glad."

She let out a short laugh. "I guess I can live with that."

"Good."

"I mean, it could be worse. At least I'm not a virgin." She smirked and gave me a small shove.

CHAPTER 19

"You let Samantha Morgan interview you? You're insane." Tess was sitting on the floor in the basement of the Bakers' house. She and Ashley had a nice spread. There were two bedrooms and a small living area. It was a little dark but comfortable. And safe.

"I thought it would be better to tell her the truth rather than have her print the rumors."

"Yeah, I get that, but why not let it all just go away?"

I thought about that. "Something you said, actually. You said I shouldn't be ashamed. It's not like I'm the only virgin in the school."

Tess shrugged. "But you don't have to make us nonvirgins feel like sluts either."

"How am I doing that? I never called anyone a slut."

"I don't think you're doing it on purpose. But that's the way it feels."

"Great."

Tess stirred the ice in her cup. "But you know, if I had it to do over again, I wouldn't have slept with Alex."

"Really?"

"Yeah. Not that I'd go announce it in the school paper or anything."

We ate dinner with the Bakers, and then Tess drove me home. My good mood dissipated the closer we got to my house. I was beyond happy that Tess and I were okay and that she was safe. But I still had a lot to deal with in my family. I knew my mom would be mad about my blowup, but I was glad I did that, too. I had gotten so used to not saying what was really on my mind that it felt good to finally let it all out.

Regardless of the consequences.

When I walked into the house, I found Mom, Dad, and Darby sitting at the kitchen table with coffee mugs in their hands.

Darby's face brightened when I came in. "Mallory, come sit with us."

I walked over but eyed my mom to see what kind of mood she was in. She looked more sad than angry, and she barely glanced up from her coffee cup as I sat down.

"We wanted to talk with you," Darby said.

Despite her smile, a shot of fear sliced through me.

"It's not healthy for us to tiptoe around one another, and I certainly don't want anyone tiptoeing around me anymore. I'm so thankful for each of you, for helping me and getting me through the last year; but it's time I stood up and became a part of this family again."

"You've always been part of this family," Mom said quietly.

"Only the part you'd let me see. I don't want to be coddled anymore. And I have Mallory to thank for that," Darby said.

Dad winked at me, and Darby squeezed my hand.

"And I've already called Brian to see if we could get together for a talk. I'm going to tell him everything, and whatever happens, happens. My past is my past. I'm not going to let it control me, but I'm not going to try and hide it anymore either. Okay?"

Her question was directed at Mom, who nodded just a little, as if it was what she was supposed to do rather than what she wanted to do. But Darby seemed to accept it.

"Now, Mallory, did you get to see Tess?"

I shared what I felt comfortable sharing, but the whole conversation was weird. Like we all weren't sure how to behave now that the old rules had been thrown aside. Especially Mom.

I woke up Wednesday morning knowing that not only would the article be out, but that I was going to have to deal with ditching school and practice.

Tess picked me up, which gave me exactly the boost I needed. I could face down the world with Tess at my side.

The school paper wasn't exactly an exciting commodity at school. I rarely even looked at it. Mostly, they just sat in piles around the building. But when we walked into school, I swear, every single person I saw had one in his or her hand. Tess snatched the last one off the floor by the door.

On the front page was a picture of me cheering. The headline read, "The Virgin Cheerleader Tells All."

Another cheerleader threw a balled-up newspaper at my face before I read the first line. Tess grabbed the paper off the floor and threw it back at her like a major-league pitcher.

"I can't believe you did this on purpose." Tess shook her head.

We walked down the hallway, where the words on the lockers were faint but still visible. Apparently permanent markers are hard to get out. The lockers would probably have to be painted over. At my locker, another word had been written over the top of *virgin*, and it wasn't a nice one.

"You're lots of things, Mallory, but you're not that." Tess pulled a marker from her bag and scribbled over the word the best she could. I opened my locker, glancing around masochistically—noticing only the scowls.

Greg walked by with a bunch of his friends, pointing at me and then at himself. He laughed as if he had done the funniest thing in the world and high-fived his friends.

"Jerks."

I closed my locker, and there was Liam.

Tess bailed. "I'll see you later."

"Hey, you." Liam had a paper in his hand. "Impressive."

"I was kind of forced into it."

Liam leaned his head and shoulder on a locker. "I'm sorry. I'm sorry. I'm sorry. I'll tattoo it on my face if it would help."

I looked into those chocolate eyes of his and decided that the more allies I had, the better. Besides, we all make mistakes, right? I stepped a little closer and brushed his hair out of his eyes. "No tattoos necessary." He tilted his head, and I smiled at him.

That was all the encouragement he needed. He slipped his arm around me and pulled me close, kissing me briefly, right on the lips.

I heard catcalls and words tossed around us, but I didn't care. For that moment it was just us.

I could almost tell whether someone was a virgin or not by how he or she reacted to me that day. Smiles = virgin. Scowls = everyone else.

I probably would have left school if it wasn't for Tess and Liam staying by my side. Before I got changed, I went to go find Tara. I was moving right along with Steps 10 and 11, and I owed Tara an apology.

She was talking with her best friend, Kasey.

"I'm sorry for missing practice yesterday. I wasn't feeling well."

Tara stood up and narrowed her eyes at me as if she didn't believe me. "Do you have a doctor's note?"

"No, I . . . uh . . ."

"Cut her some slack, Tara. It can't be easy for her right now," Kasey said. Kasey smiled at me sympathetically.

"Why should I? We all have the same rules and expectations. I don't know if she should stay on the squad at all."

I grew very still, as if any sudden movement might make her kick me off. I really loved cheerleading. I loved being on varsity and wearing my uniform and performing for the crowds. I didn't want it taken away.

Tara slammed a locker closed. "We have zero tolerance for ditching practice. You know that, Kasey." Tara stood up and pointed at me. "I don't care what kind of drama it is. Everyone has to be here every day, unless excused by a doctor. You're suspended until further notice." She stormed away, and I just stood there.

Kasey closed her locker. "I'm sorry. I'll try and talk to her."

I walked to the last bank of lockers, where Tess was tying her shoes, and dropped down next to her.

"Tara suspended me."

"What? Why?"

I filled Tess in.

"This sucks," she said. "You'll still help me with the fund-raiser, won't you?"

"Of course." I had to convince Tess not to do anything rash and just go to practice. I appreciated the solidarity, but I was secretly hoping that Tara would feel one game was punishment enough.

Liam was sitting in the lobby working on homework. He glanced up and jumped to his feet.

"You're really early. What's wrong?" he asked.

I told him what happened.

He hugged me and smiled. "Let's get out of here."

He took my hand and practically dragged me to his car. Despite me asking over and over, he refused to tell me where we were going.

I was being whisked away. I liked it.

A few minutes later he pulled into the parking lot of SkateWorld.

"Roller-skating?" I asked.

"It's like ice-skating, only warmer."

Liam got out, and I followed him to the door. "It's closed," I said.

Liam just grinned and pulled open the door.

"Now you're breaking and entering? It's closed," I repeated.

Liam turned to me. "It's fine. My friend Ben, his family owns the place. Their band practices here. Do you hear them?"

I did. He led me through the next set of doors, and the music was immediately louder.

"Liam!"

The music stopped as the three guys came over to us. Liam introduced me to Ben, who seemed like the leader; Theo, the drummer; and Matt, the keyboardist. They all seemed glad to see Liam.

"Play with us. Come on," Ben said.

"Nah. Mind if we skate, though?"

"It's all yours. Do you want some more lights on?"

"This is good."

"Okay," Ben said. "But I have the bass with me if you change your mind."

Liam laughed.

We headed to the skate rental area and picked out skates and started lacing them up. "Why don't you play with them? I don't mind watching."

Liam looked over to where the guys had started practicing again. He shook his head. "Makes me want it too bad."

He stood up, moving easily in the skates. I had roller-skated before, but it had been a few years. He took my hands and got me to my feet, then moved me out onto the floor, skating backward the whole time.

"When can you cheer again?" he asked.

"I don't know. Hopefully not too long."

"It'll be a nice break, won't it?"

"No. I don't want a break. I love cheering. I've done it forever. It's who I am."

"You're way more than that," he said. "Besides, we get to spend more time together." He stopped skating, and I rolled right into his arms. Suddenly, we could hear the guitar on the other side of the rink launch into a long solo that drew Liam's full attention.

"They asked me to join the band weeks ago," he said, watching them.

"You said no?"

"My dad would never understand. He's already upset about the college stuff, you . . ."

"Me?"

"Everything is a distraction until I choose army, navy, marines, or air force." He brushed the hair from my face. "Don't worry. I'm not going anywhere."

Liam took me home, and I was still thinking about the news that his dad saw me as a distraction. Liam's assurances did little to ease my worry.

I was going to bring up the topic again until I saw a woman getting out of a parked car. She started walking toward me, but she didn't look familiar. This woman was young, perfectly manicured, and wearing an azure business suit that looked completely out of place in our neighborhood.

Liam shut off the engine and was at my side.

"Hi, you're Mallory Dane, right?"

I nodded.

"I'm Christi Rea with Channel Four. I was interested in the piece that ran in *The Falcon's Nest* this morning."

"It's just a school paper," Liam said.

"Yes, but I'm working on a feature about sex in high schools and wanted to get your perspective on the situation."

I glanced around, and as if she could read my mind, she added, "I don't have my cameraman with me, but I would like to interview you for a segment, if you'll agree to it."

I looked up at Liam, who had his arm protectively around me. "You can say no," he said.

I heard the door open and close behind me, and turned to see Darby coming outside barefoot, picking her way across the grass to where we were standing.

"What's going on? Are you okay, Mallory?" Darby walked up and stood beside me. "Who are you?"

The woman repeated what she had told me.

"And why would Channel Four be interested in some high school story?" Darby crossed her arms and gave the woman a look that said *Convince me*.

The woman sighed and flipped open a notebook. "Stieff and Reiden just completed a study that said despite the trend of movies and books that feature teens as sexually active, current data tells them that teen sexual activity is on the decline. North County High invited an abstinence speaker to its homecoming lineup and then this." She held up one of the school papers. "It's unusual to see someone like you, by all respects a popular cheerleader, taking such a stand for abstinence."

"I'm not taking a stand on anything. That locker thing— it wasn't my idea. And that article—I was just defending myself."

"So why not share your story on a bigger level? Tell people why you chose to stay a virgin despite the pressures of high school." The woman stood there waiting.

I looked over at Darby because, without sharing her story, I could only tell part of mine, anyway. And Darby had grown very quiet. She looked back at me, but I couldn't tell what she was thinking. And I was keenly aware of Liam standing next to me as we spoke about sex.

Finally Darby spoke up. "Miss Rea. My sister and I need to talk about this. Is there a place we can call you?"

The woman whipped out a card. "My cell number is on

there. Could you let me know either way sometime today?" She left, and the three of us just stood there looking at one another.

"Well, I guess you two need to talk. I'll call you later." Liam squeezed my hand and left. I followed Darby back into the house.

"So what do you want to do?" she asked.

"Nothing," I said, shaking my head. "Things are hard enough at school."

Darby stared at the card, biting her lip. "I don't know, Mal. I kind of think we should do it."

"We?"

"Yes. We."

I dropped my bag by the stairs and followed Darby to the living room. "You're not serious, are you?"

Darby kept staring at the card and nodding. "Yes, I'm very serious."

I wasn't interested in doing any of it, but Darby seemed more determined than she had ever been. Eventually, I gave in. Darby handled calling back Christi and setting up the interview, and she was the one who told Mom and Dad what we were doing.

To say Mom was livid was an understatement. She slammed around the kitchen as if mere noise could reverse the trajectory of our lives.

"Why would you do that Darby?" *Slam!* "I can't even imagine what you think you'll get out of it." *Slam!*

I had never seen Mom so frantic. Even after Darby's suicide attempt, she was hyperfocused on not disturbing the atmosphere in any way, so slamming cabinets wasn't an option. But the idea that Darby would tell her story on television had unleashed something in my mother that was slightly terrifying.

Darby, on the other hand, was the picture of serenity. It was like watching two people you thought you knew reveal themselves to be the exact opposite.

Darby sat on a stool, a countertop separating them. "It's not what I'll *get*. It's about giving something. I didn't know until just yesterday that my fiasco kept Mallory from having sex. Think about it. It could keep other girls from doing what I did. From making my mistakes."

"Other girls are not your responsibility! It's no one's business. No one needs to hear about this." Mom moved to the counter and switched to a pleading tone. "Darling, please. Think about this. You can just move on, forget all of that ever happened. Why dredge it up?" Mom was close to tears.

"Because it *did* happen. And this amazing opportunity could help others. God can take something that nearly destroyed me and turn it into something good."

Pleading Mom switched into Angry Mom. "God? That's why you're doing this?"

"Yes. For the first time in so long, I feel like I can see things clearly. I think this is what I'm supposed to do."

"You need to think for yourself. That church isn't going to pay the price—you are." Mom started throwing dishes into the dishwasher, making it rattle.

"I am paying the price, every day. That's why I don't want anyone to go through what I've been through. There's another way."

"And what about the rest of us? You're going to drag us all through the mud!"

"I'm not dragging anyone through the mud. They were my mistakes. Not yours."

Mom grew very still, her face turned away.

A long minute later, Dad cleared his throat, making us all turn.

He didn't say anything, but he slowly walked toward Mom and wrapped his arms around her. In one swift second she melted into him, pressing her face into his shoulder. Darby got up and put her arm around my shoulder.

"I'm so scared." Mom's muffled words came from Dad's shoulder, but then she looked up at Darby, the tears falling freely. "I don't want you to get hurt. I couldn't bear to lose you."

Darby rushed to her, dragging me along, and joined in the hug. "You're not going to lose me, Mom. I promise. It won't ever happen again."

We held one another for a long time. I hadn't said a word, but I felt as if more had been accomplished in that one conversation than in all the conversations in the past year.

The news crew—well, Christi Rea and a cameraman and some guy with a bunch of lights—arrived at our house and set up everything in our living room. It wasn't live. They were taping it and would edit it with the rest of the program.

I was scared spitless. Literally. I couldn't make myself swallow, much less produce sound. I sat like a statue in the corner trying to calm down as they checked and rechecked everything.

Dad had put his foot down with Mom and insisted that we support Darby if this was what she wanted. Yet another family shift. He was with Mom in the kitchen, but I knew he'd disappear once the taping started. He didn't have the stomach, thank goodness, to sit around and watch us discuss sex with a bunch of strangers. Actually, I was pretty sure I wouldn't be speaking at all.

Darby looked calm and cool. She had already talked it out with Brian at lunch, and things had gone really well. I watched the camera guy clip a tiny microphone to Darby. She was amazing, and looked as if she had done this a hundred times before.

I slipped out onto the back porch and called Tess.

She was there within five minutes.

They were packed up and gone by eight. I seriously couldn't remember a thing I'd said. Tess and I went up to my room after it was all over.

"Was I a blathering idiot?" I asked her for the tenth time.

"No!" Tess flopped onto my bed. "But you didn't say much. You kept staring at the camera like it might grow teeth and eat you." Tess laughed, and I threw a pillow at her head.

"So I *looked* like an idiot? That's so much better."

"Trust me, no one but me would know. You did fine. Darby, though, was awesome. She's my new hero. I cannot believe she said all of that. Out loud."

"I know."

"You never answered the reporter's question," Tess said. "About it being kind of hard to have sex with someone who doesn't exist? She's right, you know. Everyone's going to wonder what you'll do now that you've got a real guy."

"It's nobody's business what I decide to do."

Tess laughed out loud. "Like that even matters."

"I mean, at least for me, nothing has changed at all. I still don't want to take the risk."

"Well, I don't think Liam will be pressuring you. You two are cute together. Makes me want to ralph."

"Gee, thanks."

"I'm just saying you'd better be careful. I mean, you're going crazy public with your chastity. Everyone will be watching."

Which made *me* want to ralph.

CHAPTER 20

And, boy, was Tess right. The newscast wasn't going to air until Friday night, but every day of school was more torture. On Thursday they announced the nominations for homecoming queen, and even though it was only for seniors, someone thought it would be funny to make a fancy sash and write THE VIRGIN QUEEN on it and hang it on my locker. On Friday I found a list of suggested male candidates for getting rid of my title. Even less funny than the sash.

My salvation was Liam and Tess. I always had someone to walk with in the hallways and to eat lunch with. It was enough to keep me afloat. Otherwise I might have hid in my room permanently.

None of it made any sense to me, though.

When I told that to Tess, she said, "It's high school, Mal. It's not supposed to be logical."

"Yeah, but who cares. Why does it even matter?"

Tess pointed a stalk of celery at me. "It's because of who you are. You defy the system."

"But I'm not the only one." I shoved my food away, crossed my arms, and pouted. I felt as if I was entitled to a good pout.

Tess put the celery down and brushed her hands together. "Okay, here's my theory. Sex is one of those things that everyone thinks everyone else is doing. Whether they've done it or not, they feel like they ought to be knowledgeable about it and at least pretend they know what they're talking about. The only people who get all 'Be pure' are the religious nuts—no offense, Liam—and since you're not one of them, Mallory, and you still don't want to have sex, well, you make no sense. You're an unknown category, and in the jungles of high school, my friend, that puts a death target on your back." Tess shrugged and took a bite of her salad.

"You think I'm a religious nut?" Liam asked.

Tess rolled her eyes. "Duh."

Liam screwed up his mouth and put his chin in his hand. "And here I was trying so hard not to be a nutcase."

"You can't help who you are," Tess said. "As for you, ride it out. People will forget all about it by the time we're seniors. Probably."

I groaned, and Liam took my hand in his. It felt warm and nice and made me almost forget everything that was happening.

For a total of two seconds. Then a group of skaters came by and suggested I come hang out with them in the parking lot to get a real education.

Tess yelled "Losers" at their backs, but I was too tired. Too tired to be strong or brave or anything at all.

I just wanted it to be over.

I couldn't watch the broadcast even if I had wanted to—which I didn't. Tess picked me up for the home game that night. Besides being freaked about the show, I was completely bummed about going to a game and not wearing my uniform. Tess seemed to think it was no big deal and that Tara would relent, so she kept chattering about the fund-raiser. I really tried to listen. The broadcast was set to air on the six-o'clock news. The game started at seven, so people would have the chance to see it before the game started.

"What if they make me sound like a nut?" I asked.

"Good grief, girl, you didn't say enough to sound like anything. Darby will get the airtime. And besides, who watches the news, anyway?"

"The smart kids."

"Well, they're probably all virgins, too. Except Cammie Herst, of course, thanks to Alex the jerk. I still can't believe him." Tess slammed the car into park. Before she jumped out she turned and looked at me. "Are you really sure about this whole thing? You don't have to be at the game. Have Liam take you to a dark movie theater where no one will recognize you."

I reassured her that I'd be fine, and she left to get ready. I knew if I just quit talking about it, it would go away and I could move on. But it all felt important somehow. As if doing this had bigger implications. I had taken a stand—a reluctant one—and I wasn't going to hide from it. I wasn't going to pretend anymore. About anything.

I went looking for Liam, who I found waiting with a Dr Pepper. He patted the seat beside him. "At least we'll get to sit together."

"As much as I like being with you, I'd still rather be down there cheering."

Liam picked up his phone, looked at the screen, and shoved it into his pocket.

"Was it a text about me?"

Liam didn't say yes, but his face told me. "What are they saying?"

"Everything from 'Way to go' to suggestions on how to get you in bed."

I cringed.

"You asked," he said. "Are you getting them, too?"

"I turned off my phone and left it at home," I said.

"That was probably smart."

I looked out at the field. It was so different from the bleachers. Instead of being up front, I was just one of hundreds. And despite wanting to be cheering and dancing, I got into the game with Liam and had fun telling him about who was on the team and which numbers they wore.

At halftime we stood in line at the concession stand and ran into Samantha Morgan.

"Hey! I saw the broadcast tonight. Nice job," she said.

"I didn't watch it."

"You're not cheering anymore?"

I filled her in on my suspension as we moved up in line.

"Aren't you the one who designs the pep rally flyers and banners?

"Yeah."

"If you're not cheering right now, do you think you could help me with something?" Samantha told us how she's been trying to figure out a way to make the newspaper more interesting and wants to redesign it. But no one on the staff actually knew how to drastically change the templates they were using. "Do you know how to do that stuff?"

"Yeah, but I'm not an expert or anything."

"Could you come to the newspaper office Monday after school and take a look at them? Please?"

I agreed. But in the back of my head I was thinking that

the plan didn't make a lot of sense, anyway. No one read the paper because it was still a physical piece of paper that you had to pick up. If she wanted people to read it, online was really the way to go.

Liam was oddly excited about it. "That would be so great if you could do it. Great college app stuff."

"I didn't say I was going to do anything. I just said I'd look at their templates."

We ordered our food and began heading back to the bleachers.

"But you never know. It might be the perfect thing for you to do."

"I don't have time for anything else besides cheering."

"Maybe that's what's great about it."

We sat down as the band was marching off the field. Liam got a phone call and left to go answer it, gesturing that he'd be right back. But as I watched him go, he looked upset. When he closed his phone, he leaned on the railing for several minutes before he came back to his seat.

"Everything okay?"

Liam sat down on the very edge of the bleacher.

"Mall, I hate to do this, but I've got to go home."

"What's wrong?"

"My dad. He got a call from my OSO. It didn't go well."

"Your OS what?"

"The recruitment guy who's been helping me with college applications and everything else. I guess I let on that I wasn't exactly sure about what I want to do."

"Oh. But that's good, right?"

Liam shrugged. "I've got to go home. He's got my mom all upset."

"Okay. Call me later?"

"Yeah." He kissed me on the cheek in a distracted way and hurried off. I wished I could help him somehow. I hadn't met his parents yet, and the little I'd heard about his dad made me scared of him. That got me wondering what my "role" was here. Was I Liam's girlfriend? We acted like a couple, but neither of us had used the words *girlfriend* or *boyfriend*.

I watched the second half of the game and the squad, but mostly I thought about Liam and his future. And my own. My parents had never pressured me to do or be anything in particular, and I had no idea what I wanted—or didn't want—to do.

Then my mind turned back to the newscast and what everyone would think. Hiding in my room the rest of the weekend would be an excellent strategy. *Maybe the worst of it will be over by Monday.*

But Tess was my ride, and she wanted to go to a party after the game.

"Your virginity is not going to make us miss our junior year, Mallory. Come on. It won't be that bad."

I really wished she'd stop using any variation of the word *virgin*. It was so awkward. "But the news show, Tess. Let me hide this weekend."

"Well, some of us don't have a boyfriend to go to homecoming with."

"Like you'll find one there?"

She screwed up her mouth and then rolled her eyes. "Better than staying in."

In my other life I would have caved and gone to the party because it was what Tess wanted to do. But now that my secrets were out in the world, I couldn't help feeling different. And hanging out at a party where half the people probably hated me (and the other half thought I was some sort of freak) was about as appealing as a visit to the gynecologist.

I looked at Tess, her eyes pleading. "I can't do it. I just want to go home."

Tess dropped me off, clearly miffed, but I knew she'd forget I wasn't with her once she got there. I called Liam three times, but he never picked up or answered my texts. I was worried, but eventually I gave up and went to bed.

I woke up the next morning thinking maybe everything that had happened in the last couple of weeks was just one big, horrible dream.

It was my blank walls that made me realize that it was no nightmare. It was my actual life.

I cautiously turned on my phone and found sixty-one texts. Some were supportive, saying they were glad I spoke up or that it made them think. Many were just names: liar and slut, to name a few. And there were two pictures sent to show me what I was missing out on. I deleted them without even opening them. I deleted everything but the kind comments—I thought I might need to read those again.

A knock at my door was followed by my dad stepping into my room. "Mally, you've got company."

I looked down at my rumpled pajamas. "Who is it?"

"He said his name was Liam."

"What time is it?"

"Nine."

"Tell him to wait. I'll be right there."

I took the world's quickest shower and made myself as cute as possible. *Liam's downstairs talking to my dad? What are they saying to each other?* I was more worried about my appearance at first, but as I finished getting ready, I started to stress.

Why is he here so early? I couldn't help but wonder if something happened when he went home. If Liam's dad saw me as nothing but a distraction . . . What if he had to break up with me? We weren't anything official, but we were *something*.

And I didn't want it to end.

Someone knocked on my door. "Mallory, come on."

It was my dad. I pulled open the door, and he was standing there with a coffee mug in his hand.

"He's still waiting, and I've run out of things to talk about. Would you please come down?"

I went to the kitchen, where Liam was sitting on one of the barstools at the counter. Waiting for me. "You okay?" I asked.

"I'm fine."

"What happened?"

He glanced around. "Can we go outside?"

I led him to the back porch, where the sun was already starting to take the chill out of the air.

He held my hand as we sat down.

"So tell me. Are they sending you away to military school?"

Liam grimaced and shook his head. "If my dad had his way, I'd be on a plane already."

The thought of Liam on a plane . . . leaving me . . . made my chest tighten and my heart actually hurt. *Is this what love feels like?*

I was almost afraid to ask any more questions. Especially with the way he was looking at me. But I had to know. "What happened?"

I could see that he didn't want to tell me either. It took him several minutes, but finally he spoke. "My dad thinks I need to simplify my life so that I can concentrate on the application process. He doesn't want me to be wasting my time on music . . . girls. . . ."

"Me?"

Liam squeezed my hand and pulled me closer. "Nothing is going to change. He may want it to, but it doesn't mean it's going to happen. I care too much about you to end this."

The reality of what he was saying sank in. His dad didn't want me around. That—combined with all the hate at school—made me want to disappear.

He lifted my head with his hand and held my gaze for a long moment. "Nothing is going to change. I think I smoothed it over for the time being."

"Smoothed it over? How?"

"By promising to be extrafocused on my applications. Promising to get in."

"But you don't want to go. . . . You didn't tell him, did you?"

He shook his head. "It'll crush him."

"So you're just going to give up on your own dreams?"

"But playing music, it's kind of a fantasy, anyway. It's not like I could make a living at it."

"Who cares?"

Liam smiled then and laughed a little. "You're good for me. So what about you? How bad is it?"

"Bad. I think I'm going to change my cell number."

"I saw your interview last night; my mom taped the

show. That was some new information . . . about your sister. How come you never mentioned it?"

I shrugged. "It was a secret. A secret I shouldn't have told."

Liam shook his head. "Don't be mad at me for saying this, but you have a lot of secrets."

"Not so many anymore."

"Tell me something. Something no one else in the whole world knows," he said.

"Why?"

"So I can prove to you that you can trust me."

"I do trust you." At least I was pretty sure I did.

"Please?"

I looked at Liam again, at his brown hair, those brown eyes—a real guy. A real guy who made a mistake but cares about me. How much I wasn't sure yet, but it was real.

Can I be strong and brave with my heart?

CHAPTER 21

Liam made me want to risk it all. Risk my heart, my emotions, everything, to find out what a real relationship looked like, felt like. But wanting to jump into a river and actually doing it were two different things. I had to jump.

Had to trust.

Liam waited patiently, stroking the top of my hand with his thumb.

"When it first happened, it was awful. We didn't even know if Darby would make it. But for me, it was worse when we got home. I felt lost and scared . . . and one night, I almost took a handful of pills myself."

Liam's eyes widened.

"It was just that one time, but I never told anyone. I don't even know why I considered it. I mean, I saw how awful it was for all of us. I wouldn't want to put anyone through what we went through. But I came close."

Liam wrapped his arms around me and pressed his face into my neck. I relaxed into his embrace, his warmth. It felt perfect.

He let me go and reached down and took his guitar out of the case.

He strummed and adjusted it, and after a little bit he looked in my eyes. "First of all, thank you for trusting me with that. And I'm so glad you're still here. Second, a secret for a secret, right? But I need to sing my secret."

I just nodded. There was no way I could get words out. He sang.

"I have been to California,
I've flown across the sea.
I've watched the sun rise up on the shore,
and seen the mountains majesty.
I've seen more beauty in this land
than I ever wished to see;
but sitting right here next to you,
well, there's nowhere I'd rather be.
Because inside all that beauty
Is a treasure deep inside.
Its worth is measured in smiles,
And I want it to be mine."

The music stopped and I stared at him, allowing a tear to drip down my face. He reached over and wiped it away.

"I didn't mean to make you cry."

I caught his hand as he brought it back down. I shook my head, feeling like I must be dreaming the moment. But the sun felt warm on my skin, and his hand was strong in mine. And I could almost still hear the music in the air. He squeezed and leaned forward.

"My secret is—I think I'm in love with you, Mallory Dane."

My heart swelled, and I couldn't speak. Couldn't breathe. He leaned forward and kissed me. Soft and sweet.

When it was over—too soon—he smiled at me and shook his head. "I have a theory about you."

"You do?"

"I don't think anyone really knows who you are. Except

maybe Tess. She might know. But everything else. I think it's all just decoration hiding the real you. I can see it in your eyes."

How could he see something like that? When I looked in the mirror, I just saw Mallory the cheerleader, the daughter, the friend. Nothing more. Just me.

"What do you see?"

"I see a girl who wants to be free."

I did want to be free. Of Todd. Of the lies. "I don't understand. I am free. Now."

"You see my dreams easily enough," Liam said. "What about your dreams?"

"I . . . I don't know."

"You must love something besides cheerleading." Liam kept strumming the guitar now and then. "Your dad showed me that photograph you took. The one in your living room? Pretty amazing."

"I guess everything has been so wrapped up with Darby, I stopped thinking about it."

"I can see that. But maybe now it's your time to find out. Brian says Darby is doing great and that her faith is strong. Don't worry. Brian's a good guy."

"I hope so. 'Cause if he hurts her, I'm coming after him."

Liam laughed.

"But you're right about Darby. She's more . . . alive . . . than I've ever seen her."

"I'll tell you another secret. Brian told me a long time ago that he wasn't going to date anyone until after he finished medical school. He wanted to stay completely focused. Then he met Darby and realized that God had other plans for him."

"You really believe God has plans for everyone?"

"Absolutely. That's why I think you should find your dreams."

"So, do you think God plans for you to be in the military? Is that the dream he put inside you?"

Liam looked like a balloon that had been popped. He stopped strumming and grew very still.

"No," he whispered. "No, it's not." He set down the guitar and put his face in his hands. "I've just been too scared to admit it. To him."

"How will he take it?"

Liam just shook his head. "It won't be pretty."

We made plans to go out that night, and he kissed me at the door, a little longer than he ever had before. I watched him climb into his car and go, then turned to see my mom leaning against the wall, watching me.

"Mom, you scared me. How long have you been there?"

She shrugged and walked into the kitchen. "Long enough." Her voice was flat. She was dressed in her yoga pants and a T-shirt. Since the interview, she had done little more than simply exist in the house with us. Darby had made several attempts to talk to her, but she still seemed unhappy. I knew, without a doubt, that I was the root cause.

I hovered nearby, allowing the physical distance to buffer me. "Mom, can we talk?"

She shrugged, and it made me ache inside. I hated that things weren't right between us.

"I'm really, really sorry. For everything. But . . . well, it's just that Darby seems really happy." I didn't add that

most of the changes that had happened were good ones—
Darby and her new joy, Dad stepping up, me not pretending
anymore.

"I know," she said, barely above a whisper.

I felt something rise up inside of me. I wasn't going to
hide anymore. I was free. And I wanted to stay that way.
"Then can you forgive me?" I asked.

Mom nodded, but it wasn't the kind of forgiveness that I
needed, the kind that would let me run back into her arms.
Then the phone rang, and anger flashed in her eyes. She
picked it up and clicked it twice to hang it up. She held out
the phone at me.

"Have you been hearing this? It hasn't stopped ringing
all morning." Mom tossed the phone onto the counter
and left.

I was relieved when Tess came bouncing through my doorway a few hours later.

"What's up with your mom?" she asked.

I rolled my eyes. "She's still upset that Darby went
public."

"Oh. Yeah. That makes sense." Tess shook her head.
"Can you still work on the posters even though you're
having mom problems?" Tess put her hands together and
gave me her puppy dog eyes.

"Of course. They're almost finished. But can you clear
the junk on my profiles? I can't bear to look at it."

Tess sat down at my computer, and after a few minutes
she looked at me. "You didn't read any of these?"

I shook my head.

"Good. I'll leave the nice ones. People are so stupid."

I cleared out the texts on my phone again. It was more of the same, but there were a few particularly nasty ones.

"Jace is saying I slept with him? Eww."

"I got that one, too," Tess said. "All done." She moved over to the cushioned bench that sat underneath my window while I sat in front of the computer to start on the poster.

"Okay, it has to pop. People have to really notice these posters," she said.

"It'll pop." I took Tess's notes and spread them out on the desk and opened my design program. Dad always bought multiple user licenses so I could use his programs. Of course, I had mostly used them for creating Todd.

I told Tess everything that had happened with Liam while I worked. Every once in a while she pointed at something for me to change.

"So then he asks me what I love and I'm, like, I have no idea and . . ."

"Can you make the date bigger?" Tess pointed at the line.

"Yeah." I highlighted it and made the font larger.

"Perfect."

"All right. Let's take this design and make a simple website so we can put it on the posters." I opened my web builder program and started transferring the design. "Anyway, I told him I didn't have any idea what my dreams were or what I'm passionate about, and . . ."

"What?" Tess stared at me as if I were crazy.

"What's wrong?" I looked at the screen, trying to figure out what she was looking at.

"What do you mean you're not passionate about anything?"

"I thought I was passionate about cheerleading, but I'm not sure about that anymore. It's really all I've done. I'm not some brainiac. I don't have any hobbies. How sad is that?"

"Duh. Yes, you do."

"No, I don't. I mean, I like cheerleading and all that, but I . . ."

"You can't be serious, Mallory."

"I'm dead serious, and he thinks . . ."

"Stop." Tess pointed at the screen. "Look at that."

"What about it?"

Tess laughed. "Mallory, that's an amazing poster, and now you're making a flipping website like you're just brushing your teeth."

I looked back at the screen, not seeing what was so amazing about it. "But that's so simple."

"For you. 'Cause you're good at it. I couldn't pull that off. Why do you think I'm always begging you to do this stuff for me?"

"So you don't have to do it."

"Well, yeah. But you're great at it. Do you like doing it?"

I sat back in my chair. "Yeah. I guess I do. It's fun to take the different elements and then layer them within the fields so that you create something completely unique."

"See? I have no idea what you're talking about. People make a living at this stuff."

I paused, and my mind drifted to Samantha and the redesign. I told Tess about it.

"You'd be perfect for that," she said.

"Really?" I spun my chair around and looked at her. "But I couldn't work at the paper and do cheerleading. Cheerleading takes up too much time, and then the weekends . . ."

"Look. Cheerleading is great and it's fun and it gives me a chance to force a little more community service into the squad. But it's not everything. It's not like either of us is planning to cheer the rest of our lives or coach or open up our own gyms. You're suspended, anyway, so it can't hurt to see if you'd like working on the paper. Maybe you can even make it into something people actually read."

I laughed, but I couldn't really argue with the logic. I had the time to explore, so why not explore? "You think the real me is a computer geek?"

"No. More like an artist but with graphics . . . and elements or whatever."

I did feel comfortable in front of my computer. "Sometimes my dad will get a client who wants really artistic photos, and he'll let me create an album of shots for them to look through."

"My point exactly. You should see your face right now. You're all lit up and stuff. As a matter of fact . . ."—Tess pulled me to my feet and in front of my mirror—"that's what passion looks like."

I squinted at myself, trying to see what Tess saw. What Liam saw. I just looked like me. But I did feel happy. Maybe I did have passion.

I couldn't wait to tell Liam.

Darby busted through my doorway before Tess and I had finished up.

"You will not believe this." Darby held out her phone. "You'll never guess who just called. Oh my, I don't know. It's crazy—I mean, like, totally crazy."

"What is it?" Tess and I asked, jumping up at the same time.

"It was a producer. For the *Mandy & More Show*," Darby said.

"I love that show," Tess said. "'Tough love for today's woman.'"

"They want to fly us to New York tomorrow to be on the show Monday morning."

"Because of . . . ," I started.

"Because of the story last night. The producer, Adrian something, must have seen it, and they were already going to do a show on talking to your teens about sex, and now they want to have us on it. Can you believe it?"

"Us?" I sank back down into my chair, suddenly feeling sick.

"You don't have to do it, but I'm going. How could I say no?"

"You just say the word *no*. It's easy. One syllable," I said.

"That would be so cool. I wanna go. I could tell them that I've decided to be totally abstinent now," Tess cut in.

"What?" I asked.

"Darby was very convincing in that interview," Tess said.

Darby grinned, her face all lit up. She really was a completely new person.

Darby walked over and sat on my bed, then turned my chair so that we were facing each other.

"Mom's already mad at me. Now she's going to hate me," I said.

Darby shook her head. "Mom's not mad at you. She's mad at herself, and me. But you didn't do anything wrong. You've done nothing but help me. Sometimes hard things are good for us. And doing the show, that's totally your call. You don't have to."

I glanced over at Tess. "Think of it as cheerleading." She clapped her hands twice and then lifted them in a pose. "Nooooo sex!"

"It's not exactly what I saw myself doing, you know?" I said.

"But that's how things happen sometimes," Darby said. "You fall into them. Think of the difference we could make, Mallory. You and me."

I took a deep breath and blew it out slowly. I was already in the middle of it all. But if I was being honest with myself, I didn't want to be. Not anymore. Step 12 was about bringing the message to others. But I couldn't do it—at least not this way.

I shook my head. "I think you're the one who can make the difference. You don't need me. I kind of want to live a normal, boring life. This is your passion, but I know it's not mine."

Darby hugged me. "You're sure?"

I nodded. "If you're okay with me not going."

"Of course. You have to do what's right for you. And I know I need to do this. Thank you, Mallory. None of this would've happened if it wasn't for you." She hugged me again and then left to call the show back.

"You just turned down meeting Mandy Oliver! You could have been the world's most famous virgin."

"I don't want to be the world's most famous virgin. I don't even want to hear that word anymore. Seriously, can we ban it from our vocabulary?"

Tess laughed. "Ours maybe, but you've already been

crowned the Virgin Queen of North County. You never know, though, maybe someone will get arrested or get caught sleeping with a teacher, and it'll deflect all the attention."

I could only hope.

CHAPTER 22

Once Tess went back to the Bakers' house, I headed downstairs to find Mom, Dad, and Darby at the kitchen table. I was not in the mood for another family meeting. I tried to sneak back upstairs, but Dad waved me over. I slipped into a chair.

Darby said, "I was just telling Mom about the show."

"I don't understand. Why can't we move on and put all this behind us? Why do you need to go on national television and tell the whole world?"

"Mom, I've told you. I think I can help others not make the same mistakes. I *need* to do this," Darby said.

"Why can't you leave it alone?" Mom looked at Darby as if she were from another planet. Totally incomprehensible.

"Why can't *you* understand?" Darby said.

Mom switched tactics. "It's too much pressure for you. The doctors told us that we have to make sure not to bring too much stress into your life. I'm trying to protect you."

"I know. I know you are. But I can handle it. I promise you."

We were all silent.

"Well, I'm not going to let you go up there alone," Mom said finally.

Dad spoke up. "I'll go with her if you want me to . . . or you can go."

Mom was quiet for a few minutes. "I'll go."

Mom and Darby were both gone by the time I woke up the next morning. I decided to tag along with Dad and go to the wedding he was shooting. Anything to avoid reality a little while longer. Things were good with Liam and Tess, but I still wasn't eager to go back to school and face anyone.

On the way, Dad called the cell company to get my phone number changed. The house phone was unplugged from the wall, but I needed my phone. I couldn't bear to look at any more evil texts. Once it changed over to the new number, I texted Liam and Tess. For the first time since the newscast, my phone finally stopped buzzing every second.

At the wedding, I watched Dad do his magic, confident and calm. It relaxed me. That was what passion looked like. Like a perfect fit. I couldn't imagine my dad doing anything but photography.

On the drive home, I asked him, "Did you always want to be a photographer?"

"When I was your age, I didn't know what I wanted to be. I had a few sales jobs, which I hated, but I always did photography as a hobby. It was your mom who talked me into doing it as a profession. I'm not sure I would've taken the risk if she hadn't."

"Why?"

Dad waved his hand, "I guess because following your dreams takes courage. I needed an extra shove."

I laughed, realizing I was more like him than I thought.

"So this Liam boy."

"Yeah."

"He seems like a nice kid."

"He is."

As soon as Tess and I walked into the school lobby the next day, we were assaulted by Greg and a bunch of his friends.

"Hey, baby!" Greg laughed, and sauntered over. "Now, why'd you go and hate on me like that? Telling people you're still a virgin after our night together?" Greg was talking loudly for the benefit of the entire lobby.

Conversations around us stilled, and people walking by slowed. I wasn't awake enough to have a showdown.

"I am a virgin. I wouldn't have sex with you for a million bucks," I said.

A murmur rose around us.

"You were the one begging," Greg said, laughing like a buffoon and fisting his friends.

I started to push past him, but he grabbed my elbow.

"I've got a smokin' video of us together."

"No, you don't." I wrenched my arm away from him and stalked off, Tess at my side, ignoring the stares around me.

"He is such a liar," I said. "I was with him for less than an hour, and all he did was eat."

Tess bit her lip.

"Tell me!"

"I got it this morning. I was hoping you wouldn't hear about it." Tess held out her phone. A video was playing, but it was small and blurry. All you could really see was a cheerleader with a guy who looked like Greg. The girl in the picture had my color hair, but it obviously wasn't me.

"That doesn't show anything."

"I know, but he's gonna say whatever he wants."

"This is never going to go away, is it?"

"It doesn't matter, Mallory. People say things all the time."

"It matters to me." At that moment I caught sight of Liam waiting near my locker. I walked straight into his arms.

"He's a liar, Liam. I didn't do anything with him."

"I know." Liam rubbed my back.

The bell rang, and I reluctantly pulled away from Liam. He kissed my cheek. "I'll see you in trig."

I saw Sophie hanging by the door of the chemistry lab, and I slowed down. She and Yvie hadn't spoken to me—just glared—since the whole Todd debacle. I circled back to Step 10 again: continuing to take inventory and making amends. And Step 11: asking God for help. *Here goes nothing.*

But as I got closer, it didn't seem like she was mad. She waved me over.

"Can we talk real quick?" she asked.

"Of course." I glanced up at the clock. "We've got two minutes. But Sophie, first, I'm really sorry for lying to you."

"Look, it's okay. I'm not mad like Yvie. I even kind of understand why you lied. I mean, I did, too. I didn't make up a boyfriend but . . . that summer? I lied about having sex."

"So you're a virgin, too?"

Sophie shook her head. "Well, I did eventually sleep with Cole. Remember him? But after seeing your sister on that newscast. Wow. Next time I'm gonna wait for someone who is really committed to me. She made a lot of sense."

"Really?" I was kind of shocked.

The bell rang, and she gave me a quick hug. "Can we be lab partners again? Hank is smart, but he's got really bad breath. I can't take it anymore."

I laughed. "Sure."

She grinned, and I followed her into the classroom.

I headed toward the newspaper office after school to meet with Samantha. Tara still hadn't reinstated me, but she'd given me a return date. I would have to miss one more game, and then I could come back.

On the way I ran into Lexi. She looked a little sad, and I instantly felt bad. Not bad enough to give up Liam or anything. But I could do something else. I could be her friend.

So I stopped and asked her how she was doing.

"Probably better than you," she said.

Before I could answer, Chad, one of Greg's football buddies, knocked my backpack off my shoulder.

"Hey!" I spun around, and he threw his arms out to the sides and took a step toward me. He was far bigger, towering over me. I refused to back down. I wasn't going to let him see how scared I was.

Lexi stepped closer, enough to let me know she was right there.

Chad pointed his finger in my face. He looked like he wanted to strangle me, but he was careful not to touch me. "This is your fault. My girlfriend suddenly doesn't want to have sex anymore."

One of the guys next to Chad chuckled, and Chad whipped out his arm and punched him in the shoulder, effectively shutting him up.

"How is that my fault?" I knew laughing would only make the situation worse, but it struck me as hysterical.

"Your stupid news show. And it's not just my girlfriend who's not putting out. You better fix this."

"Sounds to me like your girlfriend is way smarter than you."

I grabbed Lexi's arm and hurried in the opposite direction, leaving Chad to yell obscenities at my back.

"Whoa," Lexi said.

"Thanks for not bailing on me," I told her.

"What are friends for?" she said.

CHAPTER 23

It was a little pathetic, but I had to ask someone to help me find the newspaper office. A guy led me down a hallway to the very corner of the building. It was a large room with windows, and I was surprised by the number of people in there—probably a dozen or more.

Samantha came over as soon as she saw me.

"I'm so glad you could make it. I really appreciate this." She led me to a bank of computers along the wall. "You can put your stuff anywhere. I already had Drew pull up the template program for you to look at."

Drew, a nervous, skinny guy with glasses and a deep voice, pointed at one of the computers. "It's right here. The navigation is there on the left."

"Do you need anything else?" Samantha asked.

I set down my bag. "No. Let me just take a look at it."

Samantha went off to work on something else and I sat. It was a PC, and I couldn't help but notice two gorgeous, dusty iMacs sitting in a corner not even turned on. I had never used the software, but it took me only twenty minutes of playing with it to see that it was severely limited. I gave it another twenty just to see if there was anything at all I could suggest. I had nothing. They were either going to have to start from scratch or be stuck making tiny changes that no one would notice at all.

As soon as I turned around, Samantha hurried over.

"So what do you think?"

I showed her the places where changes could be made but explained how more elaborate changes weren't possible in the current program.

"InDesign would work much better for you. Do you have that software?"

Samantha looked completely deflated. "Yeah, it's loaded on the Macs I think, but everyone already knows how to use this program. Thanks for trying. I guess we just can't do it."

I stood up and glanced around the room at all the people who were completely devoted to a newspaper that I seriously wondered if anyone read.

"Have you ever thought about publishing *The Falcon's Nest* online only?"

"Yes," Drew said.

"No." Samantha glared at Drew. "It's a newspaper, not a website. People still read regular newspapers."

I resisted asking her how she knew that. "Does everyone feel that way?" I glanced at Drew, who didn't look like he was going to speak up again.

"You're not the first person to suggest it, if that's what you're asking," Samantha said.

That *was* what I was asking. "It would be worth considering. There's a reason why so many print mags and papers have been moved online. You can have fresher content, and it's more accessible." I was pretty sure Samantha wasn't buying it. "Look, just think about it. If you switch to something like InDesign, the paper could be redesigned the way you really want it. At least online."

"Thanks for your help," Samantha said again, and I knew

I was getting the brush-off. I grabbed my bag, surprised at how disappointed I was. I had only been doing a favor. This wasn't my world, so why did it matter to me?

As I walked home, I couldn't help planning what I would do if she'd given me the chance. By the time I got home, my head was so full of ideas that I had to put them somewhere. So I fired up my computer and went to work. Maybe if I showed Samantha what I was talking about, she'd get excited about it.

At the very least, it helped me avoid the world and homework a little longer. I had a working web layout of *The Falcon's Nest* by eight.

When I finally wandered downstairs to find some food, Liam and Brian were at the counter talking with my dad. Huh? It was at once both so bizarre and so comforting that I had to stop and take it in. Liam looked up and smiled—the kind of smile that you know is meant only for you.

"You're ignoring your phone." He raised his eyebrows at me.

"Sorry. But it's your fault."

"How could it be my fault?"

"You were the one who was all 'explore the possibilities.'"

"The newspaper?" he asked.

I took him upstairs to show him the layout and told him my plan to try and convince Samantha and the newspaper staff to go to a web-only version. "Not only is it environmentally friendly, but I think people would actually read it if we could deliver the content in multiple ways. Don't you think?"

"*I'm* convinced." He laughed. "And I've never seen you so excited about something. Definitely a side of you I like." He took my hand and pulled me and my chair closer to where he was sitting.

"I have some news, too."

"Oh, yeah?"

"I got a nomination to attend the naval academy."

I frowned. "Is that good news?"

"No, but I told my dad that I didn't want to go there or join any branch of the military."

"You did!" I hugged him but sat back quickly. "What happened?"

"Let's put it this way—I'm living with Brian at the moment."

I covered my mouth with my hand. "That bad?"

Liam nodded. "Yeah. But I feel so relieved, I swear I could fly. I didn't know how much it was holding me down until it was finally out in the open."

I could relate to that.

He rubbed the top of my hand and smiled at me.

"What are you thinking?" I asked.

"I'm thinking that I'm just beginning to know who you are, Mallory Dane."

"Maybe I am, too."

He laughed at that and then leaned in and kissed me. Total perfection.

"Wait!" I jumped up and grabbed my camera from my dresser. "We need a picture." I put my cheek next to his, held out the camera, and snapped our picture.

No Photoshop necessary.

A few minutes later we heard voices downstairs. That meant Mom and Darby were home. I squeezed Liam's hand before we went to join them.

The first thing I noticed was the laughter. Darby was in Brian's arms, and my mom was smiling—something I hadn't seen since that day they went to the mall.

Mom caught my eye, walked over to me, and wrapped me in a hug. I stayed there soaking it in until she leaned back with her hands on my shoulders.

"I'm sorry, Mallory. I took out my frustration on you, and it wasn't fair. You're right. Darby's happy. And I want that for you, too."

She hugged me again.

Dad made everyone come into the living room, and the six of us sat around and listened to Darby tell us everything that had happened on the show. Every time I saw a smile spread across her face, it caught me off guard. This was a new Darby. It was pretty amazing to see.

Once Liam left and I assured Tess that I wasn't dead, I was drawn back to my computer. I kept rearranging the placements, trying to get a feel for the best way to arrange the content. I used the paper with my interview as a guide for what kind of features they typically had. The website had so many possibilities that I wasn't sure how far to go with it.

Just as I was heading to bed, Darby knocked lightly on my door and stepped inside.

She grinned. "I didn't want to say it in front of everyone until I talked to you. The studio has been fielding phone calls from agents and publishers all day. They want us to write a book."

"Us?"

"Well, I know you didn't want to do the interview, but your story, well, it's a part of my story now. I couldn't do it without sharing your part of the story."

"Share away."

"You still don't want to be involved?"

I shook my head. "No. But I'll help you in any way I can. Maybe I could design your logo and website."

"My logo and website?"

"Yeah. You need a name for what you're doing. Like that Barbara chick who came to my school. If you're gonna write books and go around and speak and all of that, you'll need a really cool website and brochures and stuff."

Darby sat on my bed. "I didn't even think about that, but you're right."

"Things with Brian look good, too."

"Things with Brian are wonderful. It's still awful about . . ."—her voice caught in her throat—". . . the baby thing, but the doctors didn't say it was impossible. Brian says he's thrilled as long as he has me. Isn't that sweet?"

"Pretty sweet."

"And you and Liam?"

"It's good. Undefined. But good."

Darby fell back on the bed, her hands on her head. "It's all happening so fast."

"But you can do it, right?" I thought she could.

"With God, all things are possible," she said.

I had a feeling that Darby and God would make a pretty good team. Me, I was just glad to have my sister back.

At school I ignored all the jeering. It was sad that this had become the norm.

I enlisted Tess and Liam to help me take an informal poll about the school newspaper. At lunch we sat together and tallied our results.

"I asked thirty-eight guys today. Twenty of them didn't read it, fifteen didn't even know we had a school newspaper, and three were confused by the question," Liam said. He was eating fried chicken again. He held out a leg. "You'll try it one of these days."

"Ew, slacker," Tess said. "I talked to sixty-three people."

"How is that even possible?" Liam asked.

"I'm incredibly efficient. Twelve said they read it but only the front page. The rest either didn't read it or didn't know about it. And two art students confessed to stealing the stacks for projects."

"Same here," I said. "Of course, I could only ask the people who would actually talk to me."

"It'll stop eventually," Tess said. "Everything does. When are you going to talk to Samantha?"

I held up my thumb drive. "After school."

It bothered me how nervous I was as I walked to the newspaper office. If they didn't want to do it, so what? But at some point, while sitting in front of my computer imagining the possibilities last night, it had started to matter a lot.

Samantha looked up from a desk when I stepped into the doorway.

"Hey, Mallory."

"Can I show you something? It won't take long. I promise."

She nodded, and I went back to one of the Macs and turned it on. I popped in the thumb drive and pulled up the web pages I had designed. Samantha put on her glasses and watched over my shoulder, leaning in as I ran the slideshow of pages.

She began asking questions, and after an hour of explaining how it worked and what they could do, she sat down and frowned.

She still seemed skeptical, so I decided to push harder and tell her about the poll. "A lot of the students we talked to don't read the paper. But they should, and this is just a different way to deliver it to them. What's more important: having it in paper form or having students read it?"

She kept frowning, and I couldn't figure out what she was thinking. Then she suddenly stood up and called the staff over to the computer. My stomach churned as she scrolled through the pages for everyone in the room to see.

"She said they're going to talk about it as a team and decide." I climbed into Liam's car.

"So you're offering to run the whole web portion for them?"

I paused. "I guess I am."

Liam pulled out of the parking lot. "What about cheerleading?"

"I don't know. Tara said I can go back next week."

"If you do both I'll never see you."

"Well, I don't even know yet if Samantha will agree to it."

Liam shrugged. "Why wouldn't she? Newspapers are archaic. They should have done it years ago. But we're both going to be busy because—I joined Ben's band. I'm going to have rehearsals and who knows what else."

"You did? Liam, that's awesome, but . . . what about your dad?"

Liam shook his head. "I didn't even tell him. But my mom's excited for me. I'm not sure where my dad's head is at right now. He hasn't talked to me at all since I moved in with Brian."

"Maybe he'll come around."

"So you're okay with having a boyfriend in a band?"

"Did you just define our relationship?"

Liam looked confused. "What do you mean?"

"You said *boyfriend*."

He crinkled up his eyebrows. "What else would I be?"

"I just wasn't sure."

He seemed to get it finally. "Mallory, would you be my girlfriend, and will you go to homecoming with me?"

I laughed out loud and leaned over and kissed him. "Yes and yes. I thought you'd never ask."

I noticed the news van as soon as Liam turned onto our street. Darby had said something about the local news, and I spotted Christi Rea on the porch with her crew hauling lights inside.

I promised to call Liam later and climbed out of the car. Christi held out her hand when I got to the porch.

"Good to see you again. Your sister said she didn't think you'd be joining us today. It's just a quick follow-up to everything that's happened since her New York trip."

"I think Darby can handle it. But I do have a favor to ask. My friend Tess is having a toy drive in November for the local domestic violence shelter. Do you think you could let people know about it? If you mentioned it on air, it would really help." I pulled out a flyer from my bag and handed it to her.

"Sure. We could probably do that. And I'll make sure it goes on our website, too."

"Really? Thank you, that would be so great."

"Always willing to help a good cause," Christi said. "I'd better make sure we're all ready in here." She shook my hand again. I reached for my phone to call Tess, then stopped.

I'd let the news coverage be a surprise.

CHAPTER 24

Within the first hour of school the next day, Samantha had said yes to the redesign, and Tara asked me to come back and cheer for the game on Friday. Tess told me it was because Pia sprained her ankle and couldn't stunt.

Liam laughed. Which was completely unhelpful.

"So now I either have no life or I have to choose?"

"Were you cheerleading because you love it or because it's fun to do?" Liam put his arm around my shoulder. It distracted me from his question.

Here I was, walking down the hallway at school with a guy. A real boyfriend. Such a strange thing. I still couldn't believe it.

Maybe I don't have to choose. The fall cheering season was only a few more weeks. So, with the redesign, cheering, and the fund-raiser, it would be an intense few weeks, but it was possible. Wasn't it?

Liam stopped me and led me over to an empty doorway.

"I need to tell you something," he said, a nervous look on his face.

I couldn't help it—my heart sank. It was bad news whatever it was.

"I was talking to Ben last night at rehearsal about the stuff they already have booked, and I . . . well, I messed up the dates."

"What dates?"

"That concert I told you about? I thought it was the week before homecoming, but it's . . . the same night."

"So . . ."

"So I can't take you to homecoming. I feel awful, but it's too late to change it and . . ." He sighed heavily.

I was quiet. I knew how important the band was to him. And really, it was just a silly dance. But it was my first homecoming with a real boyfriend, and now I was going to miss it.

As disappointed as I felt, though, I knew what I needed to do.

"Well, you have to do the concert," I said.

"I feel terrible."

"Don't. It's not your fault. And it's just a dance."

"I'll make it up to you," Liam said.

I smiled. "Oh, I know you will. And I already have an idea."

He grinned and kissed me. "Lay it on me."

At lunch we sat with Tess, who was completely distracted. She had thrown herself into prepping for the fund-raiser, a not-so-veiled attempt to avoid her life at home, which was both better and more difficult at the same time. With social services involved, Tess was getting frustrated with having to deal with so many other people.

I hated that it was still a bit of a wedge between us.

But I also thought that if I could just get her through the fund-raiser, we could deal with it afterward.

"So," I started. "I was thinking Liam's band could play

at the fund-raiser. Christmas music would add a nice atmosphere and—"

"They'd do that?" Tess interrupted.

Liam said, "We wanted to see what you thought before I asked them."

"Yes. Go call. Now. That would make the event so much more epic."

Liam took out his cell phone and walked away.

"You okay?" I asked.

Tess poked at her food. "What am I going to do with myself when this is all over?"

"Probably find some other crazy project," I said.

"They want us to do family counseling with my mom."

"Maybe that will be a good thing."

"I'm just so mad at her. And I don't want to sit around talking about it." Tess sat up and gestured with her chin, signaling that Liam was back.

"Ben's checking with everyone else, but he sounds stoked about it. He wants to know if we can advertise the event."

"Advertise away." Tess launched back into planning mode. "Okay, so I drew a layout of what I'm thinking we're going to do with the space. They won't let us move in until Saturday morning, so we'll only have a few hours to get ready. We need more help."

Tess unfolded a piece of paper and took charge.

Later I walked down to the newspaper office to let Samantha know that I'd do the redesign but that I'd have to work from home until cheerleading ended. She was fine with it. I was relieved to hear that she wanted to launch in January, because that gave me more time.

"Before you leave I wanted to run something else by you."

"Sure." I glanced at the clock; I could spare five minutes if I sprinted to practice.

Samantha walked to her desk, and I followed.

"You said we're going to have a lot more space to fill, so I wanted to see if you would do a weekly column—starting in January, of course."

"A column? I'm not really a writer."

"I think you could manage this. Your story made me think about how everyone has their own secrets, and it's the secrets that make us think we're all alone, that no one else in the whole world could understand how we feel. What if you did a 'High School Confessional' column and let people anonymously share their secrets?"

"So it would be other people's stories?"

Samantha nodded and adjusted her glasses. "I think it could be really eye-opening. And if you rewrite their stories in your own writing voice, then it would protect their privacy while at the same time letting others know they aren't alone."

"How am I supposed to get people to share their secrets?"

"You don't have to convince them. Look." Samantha handed me a stack of papers. "We've been getting these ever since that article ran about you. And always in hard copy— I'm assuming it's because no one wants their e-mail traced."

I took the papers and began reading:

I've been stealing since I was 6 years old. I know it's wrong, but I can't stop. I think I need help, but I'm afraid to ask.

My dad just lost his job again, and I think we're really going to lose our house this time.

I feel like everyone in this school hates me.

The guy I've been in love with for the past three years doesn't even know I exist. Maybe that's why I can't let go.

I didn't stop until I had been through the whole stack. Even then I wanted to start over. I had no words.

"I know. I felt that way, too. You could take a secret, rewrite it, and then respond to it in some way. Point them in the right direction. What do you think?"

In the same way that I knew interviews were not for me, I knew this *was*. This was my Step 12.

Life became a blur, and I was too busy even to care that I was still being propositioned in the hallway—usually by Greg and his friends—or getting scowls here and there. I accepted the title of the Virgin Cheerleader. I was going to have to live with it.

We spent hours putting up flyers and working out a thousand little details for the fund-raiser, so I didn't have much time to feel sorry for myself. But I found myself a little sad during the homecoming parade and game, because everyone was talking about the dance.

Tess got asked to the dance several times. But in her solidarity with me, she opted not to go so she could come to Liam's concert.

Tess picked me up even though Brian and Darby were going to the same place. Liam was playing at some big youth event. His whole church was going—maybe his mom, too.

I finally settled on my best pair of jeans, knee-high boots, and a belted sweater that was new. I had to go back inside to grab my camera bag because I had promised to record the event for Liam.

I was out of breath by the time I settled in the Jeep next to Tess.

"Got everything this time?"

"I think so."

"It will be fine. Meeting the parents is never as bad as you imagine it."

"Not sure that helps."

"Well, imagine trying to introduce a guy to my mom. Hmmm, should I try when she's drunk or hung over?"

"Liam's already met my mom and dad, but it's because he keeps coming over. Which is nice."

"Yeah, you should keep him."

I hoped so. I had no idea what a long-term relationship would look like. But it felt good to try.

We arrived an hour before Liam's band was supposed to play. The place was already packed. It was at a church, but they had moved all the chairs so everyone was mingling in a wide-open space. The lights were down, and colored lights swirled around the room. It wasn't homecoming, but it looked fun. Plus, I was here with my best friend, and my boyfriend was in the band. Not too shabby.

The low light wasn't ideal for taking pictures, so I spent some time adjusting the settings on my camera.

Then I told Tess I was going to look for Liam. *My guy.* I liked the sound of that.

I headed for a door near the stage, but a tall, skinny boy with jet-black hair stopped me.

"Sorry. Band only."

"I'm with the band," I told him.

He looked me up and down, then shrugged and let me through. I followed the music and found them all in a classroom warming up. Liam grinned and set down his guitar when he saw me. I said a quick hello to the other guys and got a kiss from Liam.

I took some pictures of them all together and got a few of Liam warming up. I loved how he looked when he was concentrating.

When a girl opened the door and yelled "Five minutes!" into the room, everyone started gathering their stuff and leaving. Liam got his guitar and put his arm around me as we walked from the room. In the hallway, we saw a woman with reddish hair and glasses. She looked nervous, but she smiled when she saw Liam. He grabbed her in a hug.

She seemed relieved by his reaction.

"Mom, this is Mallory."

I held out my hand, but she hugged me instead. "I've heard a lot about you."

"Dad's not here." Liam said it more as a statement than a question. She shook her head and folded and refolded her gloves.

"He wanted to, but he couldn't get away."

Liam drew his lips in a tight line. "I really think it would help if he could see for himself . . . never mind. I have to get ready. I hope you enjoy it, Mom." Liam waved and ran off, leaving me standing there with his mom.

"I guess we better go on in," I said to her.

"Yes, I should find Brian. I believe he's already here."

It was only a minute or so before we reached the crowded room. I spotted Brian and Darby toward the back and pointed them out to Liam's mom. She squeezed my arm and leaned in toward my ear to say thank-you.

It took me a lot longer to find Tess, and by the time I did, someone was onstage introducing the event.

Tess pulled me toward a far wall where it was a little easier to talk. "So?"

I shrugged. "I met his mom. It was quick, and she seemed . . . uncomfortable."

"No Dad?"

"No, and Liam seemed upset."

Tess pointed. The band had just come onstage. "He looks okay now."

And she was right. Liam's grin was back as he messed with his guitar and microphone. We listened as Ben introduced the band and explained the long story behind their name: The Yellow Turnips.

"He'll be all right. Look at how things turned out for Darby."

"True."

With a loud opening, they began to play a song that I wasn't familiar with. It was really catchy. The crowd loved it, and I felt this swell of . . . pride, I guess. That was Liam up there. My boyfriend.

Liam's dad was missing out. But maybe he'd realize that eventually.

The band played several sets of music, and in between they had different speakers. I snapped tons of pictures, more of Liam than of anyone else; but I got some good ones of the whole band as they played and sang. I got some great crowd shots by climbing onto a stack of chairs. I was already thinking about the cool posters I could make them for their next concert.

Ben was one of the speakers. He talked about the band's spiritual roots and even mentioned abstinence. It felt nice to be someplace where I didn't feel so odd and out of place.

I looked over to where Brian was standing with Darby,

his arm around her shoulder, and refocused the camera to snag the shot. I looked at it on the camera and stared.

If I didn't know any better, I'd say my big sis was falling in love.

CHAPTER 25

After the concert it was one long push to the day of the fund-raiser.

Darby, Dad, and I got up crazy early so that we could load the SUV with all the camera equipment and get to the warehouse in time to set up everything.

We were still loading the backdrops when Mom came down all dressed. She poured herself a cup of coffee.

"Why are you up so early, honey?" Dad asked.

She took a sip and shrugged with one shoulder. "I figured we had to leave early." She picked an apple from the basket on the counter and took a bite. "You do need help, don't you?"

"The more the merrier," I said.

My mom was definitely still struggling with all the changes in our family, but I knew it was only because she was scared. Scared of losing Darby, me—all of us.

I could understand that. The pictures in my head from that day were still crystal-clear, but I believed Darby had changed. It wasn't just that she had a new guy or that good things were happening. It's that Darby was different, deep in her soul.

When we arrived at the warehouse, we immediately set to work setting up the photo station. Both Liam and Brian came over to say hello, but Tess shuttled them to the stacks of tables so they could start setting up.

It took us a while, but once Dad made it to the point where he was just checking his lighting, I went to find Tess. She was pacing in a corner chewing on her fingernail and staring at a clipboard.

"What can I do?" I asked.

"I don't know. I don't know! I feel like I'm forgetting something major."

I looked around at all the volunteers. Liam and Brian were setting up rows of tables for the donations to be checked in and sorted. Ben and the other guys from the band were setting up the music equipment. Santa was chatting with my dad. There was plenty of space for everything.

"I don't think it's possible that we forgot anything. Everything will be perfect," I said.

Katie came running over to Tess. "Some people are at the door who are headed out of town, so they want to drop off their donations early. What should I tell them?"

Tess went from frazzled and worried to calm and collected in less than a second. "Tell them to bring them in. We have a station already set up here, so if you don't mind going through the stuff, . . ." Tess walked off with Katie.

I went back over to my dad. I turned on the computers and pulled up my files. I was so glad to have a computer job. Tess had agreed that the elf costume would be wasted on me if all I was going to do was sit there and work with photos. I had designed three different frames for the Santa pictures. After my dad took the digital shot, I could position the picture in the frame and print it out. It would cost us less than two dollars for an 8 by 10, but we were charging ten dollars. That allowed us to have a profit to buy the uniforms but was still cheap enough to make them affordable.

Mom pulled up a chair next to me. "Did you make those?" she asked.

"Mm-hmm. They choose the design from these printed samples."

"You're so much like your dad," she said.

"Thanks."

"Mallory. This last year, well, I feel like I was so worried about Darby that I forgot to watch out for you."

"I'm okay."

"I know, but I want you to know that I'm here, and that I'm going to try harder."

"You know, I didn't mean for any of it to happen the way it did. But . . ."

"But things turned out pretty well," she finished. "I guess . . . change is hard for me, and we had a system. Even though the system wasn't working—for any of us." She wrapped her arms around me and pulled me close. "I'm so proud of you—you know that, don't you?"

"I do now."

"Excuse me? We've got people lining up here, ladies," Darby scolded us playfully.

Mom smiled at me the way she used to, and I felt all cozy inside. She stood up. "I guess we better get busy then."

And we did. Darby and Mom handled the order forms and the money while Dad and I handled the pictures and printing. We worked as a team, and every once in a while I'd look around at Mom or Darby or my dad and allow myself a moment of amazement that we had come so far.

Liam and the guys made everything Christmasy with

the music, and they got a bunch of kids to dance to "Jungle Bell Rock." I tried to watch and make sure Tess was okay, but she was in her in-charge mode, and even I wasn't going to mess with that.

We had to stay open nearly two hours later than we'd planned because of the sheer amount of people who came by. We received unbelievable donations. Once we had packed up the equipment and tables, we looked out over the mounds of toys, many of them brand-new.

Tammy, the woman who ran the shelter, shook her head. "Way more than what we need at Hope House. But I can already think of more places that could use some presents for families. I'll start making some calls."

We had a week in the building to get all of the toys distributed, so I knew we had time to find a place for everything. We were going to make a lot of kids happy.

Tess came over, the clipboard now gone and happy exhaustion on her face. "Hey, how much money did we make?" she asked.

"Three times what we need for the uniforms."

"Good. Then we can give it to Hope House or even the homeless shelter. . . ."

"Tess. We already voted on what to do with the extra money."

"Who voted? Nobody told me about a vote." Tess put her hands on her hips.

"The whole squad." I waved the girls over. "We want you to have it."

"No way. I can't do that."

"Yes, you can. And you won't argue with us," I said.

Tess pressed her hand to her mouth, and tears welled up in her eyes. The squad surrounded Tess, clapping, hugging, and encouraging her.

When they dispersed and it was just the two of us again, I handed her the envelope of money.

"How did you . . . ," she started.

"The Bakers told me that you've got a stack of medical bills for your mom at home, and I know it probably won't solve the whole thing, but it will help. No one knows the details—I was very careful. But when I said you needed some help, it was unanimous."

"I don't know what to say."

"Don't say anything."

"So now I'm a charity case?" she said.

"Look at it this way. At least you're not the Virgin Queen of North County."

"Good point." She laughed.

I joined in, realizing that Tess was right again.

The whole thing was kind of funny. Now.

SECRET HIGH SCHOOL

By Mallory Dane

I'm Mallory. Most of you know me as the Virgin Cheerleader. But it turns out I'm not the only one with a secret.

Secrets have a way of isolating us and making us feel like we're all alone. But we usually aren't. Many times there are other people, maybe even sitting right next to you in class, who know exactly how you feel.

So this space is for you. To start being honest. To start being real about who you are and what you have to deal with. Sometimes that's all it takes to get us going in a new direction.

You already know my secret.

What's yours?

www.secrethighschool.com

If you or anyone you know is thinking about suicide, please call **1-800-SUICIDE** to talk to someone who can help you right now.

You are not alone.